Harriet Maria Gordon Smythies

Guilty; Or, Not Guilty

Vol. 1

SALZWASSER VERLAG

Harriet Maria Gordon Smythies

Guilty; Or, Not Guilty

Vol. 1

Reprint of the original, first published in 1864.

1st Edition 2022 | ISBN: 978-3-75259-391-4

Verlag (Publisher): Salzwasser Verlag GmbH, Zeilweg 44, 60439 Frankfurt, Deutschland
Vertretungsberechtigt (Authorized to represent): E. Roepke, Zeilweg 44, 60439 Frankfurt, Deutschland
Druck (Print): Books on Demand GmbH, In de Tarpen 42, 22848 Norderstedt, Deutschland

GUILTY; OR, NOT GUILTY.

GUILTY; OR, NOT GUILTY.

A NOVEL.

BY

MRS. GORDON SMYTHIES,

IN THREE VOLUMES.

VOL. I.

LONDON:

1864.

GUILTY, OR NOT GUILTY.

CHAPTER I.

> "Oh! the heart, like a tendril,
> Accustomed to cling,
> Will twine round the nearest
> And loveliest thing."
>
> MOORE.

THE Countess of Rockalpine sat in her elegantly-furnished dressing-room in Park Lane. The soft light of an afternoon in May stole in through the tinted plate-glass, the rose silk and white lace curtains, and the flowers that filled the balcony. The large oval mirror, draped with lace and muslin, looped up with pink ribbons, reflected a still lovely face. It would have been lovelier, perhaps, but that

Art had vainly tried to supply the lilies and roses of youth; and a good deal of real beauty —autumnal beauty—thus acquired an artificial gloss, which threw a doubt on what *was* real. Cosmetics of every description covered the toilet-table, mixed with jewelry, combs, brushes, and every kind of elegant trifle. The Countess was still handsome, fascinating, thoughtless, vain, and romantic; she had been much handsomer, much more fascinating, but not more vain, thoughtless, and romantic, when, some twenty-three years before, she had been offered up at the altar of St. George's, Hanover Square—a sacrifice to Mammon, in the shape of the cold, stern, rather bald, rather grey, rather elderly, but very wealthy Earl of Rockalpine.

It is a very common sacrifice. At that altar, in her first bloom, crowned with orange-blossoms, veiled and robed in white, were sacrificed the Maiden, Love, Liberty, and

Hope, for realities of twenty thousand a year, a countess's coronet, a mansion in Park Lane, Rockalpine Castle, Beech Park, an equipage, an opera-box, and a handsome settlement. Once his, the Earl, who was a proud and disappointed man—having vainly aimed at political influence and senatorial fame, as a Tory of the old school—took her to Rockalpine Castle, and wanted her to live there almost entirely. There *he* was a great man—a solitary star! In London he was only a twinkling light in one of many constellations.

Rockalpine Castle, stern, grey, and bald as himself, was also alone in its grandeur. Hauteville House, Park Lane, was one of numberless town mansions of equal or greater importance.

The bride was timid, and sighed in heart over her enforced seclusion and solitude. Two sons were born to her in the course of three years, and when they left the nursery and her empire, to cheer her life a little, she adopted and educated as her own *protegée* the beautiful Clarissa Croft, daughter of the lawyer who was the Earl's agent at Rockalpine Castle. It never struck the Countess, for she was thoughtless, nor the Earl, for he was all pride and disdain of humbler people, that Clarissa—a perfect sunbeam of brightness and beauty flitting about the old grey castle—might become a peril and a temptation, in after years, to those young scions of so proud a house.

The bride had been timid and complying—the wife soon had a will of her own. The pleasures of the season in London, which she had resigned in her youth, she resolved to enjoy when she grew older and, as she said, wiser. And now she was forty, and her sons were with her in town. The elder, Lord Hauteville, was twenty-two; the second was a year younger. Clarissa, still by her side, was about nineteen.

The five o'clock tea, so universal with fine ladies, was served in the Countess's boudoir. Clarissa presided at the tea-table, and Lord Hauteville and his brother both dropped in, each thinking to steal a march on the other; for both were desperately in love with Clarissa—the elder, with that pure love which a maiden glories to inspire—the younger, with that fierce selfish passion which she blushes to awaken.

"Show Hauteville and Wilfred our dresses for to-night, Clary," said the Countess. Lady Rockalpine and her *clique* were trying to revive the palmy days of Almack's. Clarissa rose and left the room.

"Are you going to take Clarissa to Almack's, mamma?" asked Wilfred.

"Yes! as a lady patroness *I* can give her a voucher; and I'm sure she'll be the belle of the room. Nay, more, I think I shall present her at the next Drawing-room."

"Dear, kind mamma!" said Lord Hauteville; and he blushed with delight, for he thought that everything that raised Clarissa in the social scale removed a barrier to his honourable hopes.

"It would be very rash, I think, and might give offence in high quarters. An attorney's daughter!" said Wilfred, growing pale; for the better Clarissa's position in society, the less likely was he to succeed in degrading her.

"An attorney's daughter," said the Countess, "but *my* friend."

Clarissa came in, followed by Finette and Bobbin, who displayed the Countess's gold brocade, and Clarissa's tulle, looped-up with apple-blossoms; the gorgeous head-dress of the patroness, the apple-blossom wreath of the *protegée*. The Countess was very amiable;

she took the greater interest in Clarissa's dress, and, sooth to say, so did her sons.

"Now go to bed till it is time to dress," said the Countess to Clarissa; "you have dined early; I shall dine at Lady Lofty's grand dinner-party, and come home to dress for the ball. Go fairly to bed till ten, Clary; that is what the De Bolton girls, the Marchelles, the Demodes, and all the young Hebes of fashion do."

"But I am not tired, my lady, and I am no Hebe of fashion."

"You shall be henceforth; so do as I bid you."

Clarissa obeyed, and the Countess was right; it is thus that girls in the *beau monde* contrive to look fresh night after night during the season, and yet to polk till three or four in the morning.

A new cosmetic and a new corset enabled the Countess (as Wilfred in his Oxford slang said) to *take the shine* out of all the wall-flowers.

Clarissa was the *belle* of that, her first and last, ball.

By the evening of the next day the Countess lay a corpse in Hauteville House! The cosmetic contained a preparation of lead, fatal to human life, when used as she had done it, to whiten her face, arms, and bust. The tight corset had probably aided its evil effects. She had always hated the thought of Death—wills, legacies, &c. Clarissa was unprovided for. Hauteville House, Rockalpine Castle, Beech Park, were no longer homes for her.

She was in deep grief, and a stepmother reigned in her father's home.

An aunt gave her a temporary shelter in town, and she intended going out as a companion or a governess, when her health and spirits recovered from the blow to her affections, and the ruin of her fortunes. Both brothers obtained access to her. The one was but too welcome; the other, but that he was feared, would have been shunned! Clarissa did not go out into the cold, cold world to gain a living after all! And why? Her aunt could not maintain her. Wilfred felt there was some mystery, but he could not fathom it!

He felt, too, that his attentions, his visits, were unwelcome, and this knowledge only increased his passion.

Sometimes Clarissa went into the country, with her aunt, for months together, and then returned to town, her bloom improved, her spirits cheerful, her beauty greater than ever.

She was in Charlotte Street, Fitzroy Square, when her two lovers were summoned to Rockalpine, for the Earl required their presence there.

Both were very regretful at leaving London, but only one was regretted.

CHAPTER II.

"Oh! Love, what is it in this world of ours
That makes it fatal to be loved? Ah! why
With cypress branches dost thou wreathe thy bowers,
And make thy best interpreter a sigh."

BYRON.

THERE was a solemn stillness on the purple moors, and in the dark pine-woods of the Rockalpine estates in Northumberland. The slanting rays of the setting sun came down alike on the black spiral tops of the tallest fir-trees of the forest, and on the pink bells of the heather.

A wild brook gleamed like molten gold in those rays; they gilded the grey battlements of the old castle on the heights, flamed and flashed from the windows of the villa of the agent of the lord of that castle, and lighted up the humble roof of the poorest tenant on the estate.

It was a lovely autumnal evening; there was not a creature to be seen, not a sound to be heard, save the distant lowing of the cattle, and the buzz and hum of the insects in the grass.

The moon, wan, dull, and out of place, like an actress by daylight, was looking from her cold grey abode, pale with envy at the radiant *coucher* of the monarch of day—the gold, the purple, and the crimson of his canopy and couch.

Suddenly, a young and very handsome man, in shooting costume, gun in hand, and a dog by his side, bounded lightly across the brook, and entered the wood. His noble and delicate features, fair waving hair, and princely bearing, betokened some one of importance; but yet no gamekeeper attended him, and he had thrust some grouse he had shot into the pockets of his shooting-jacket.

As he passed through the wood, with a birr and a whirr, up rose a noble cock-pheasant; bang went the sportsman's gun, and a quivering bleeding mass of green, purple, and gold, lay at his feet. The sportsman picked up the pheasant—habit hardens the softest heart—he who had just before stepped aside not to harm the beetle in his path, felt no pity for the regal bird.

He walked on musingly, and re-loaded his gun, and the word "Clarissa," which was engraven on his heart, rose to his lips, when suddenly a shot startled him.

The blood flew to his noble face. "Poachers, no doubt," he said to himself; and without one thought of peril, or one feeling of fear, he rushed forward in the direction whence the shot came. "Hallo! Wilfred," he said, recognising his brother, like himself, alone and unattended; like himself, gun in hand, and laden with game; like himself, having just re-loaded his gun. "What brings you here, Wilfred?" he asked, good-humouredly.

"I might ask the same question of you, Hauteville," replied the younger brother, livid with some strong, secret emotion; "only that I can answer that question as well as you can."

"What are you driving at?" said the elder brother (Lord Hauteville, heir of the title and estate of Rockalpine).

"At your secret idol, the hidden Ida of your breast, Hauteville—Clarissa!"

Hauteville blushed like a girl; he laughed, and said,

"Nonsense! what has Clarissa" (he spoke the name with the trembling tenderness of love), "what has *she* to do with my taking a stroll through the woods on this fine afternoon, and shooting a brace of pheasants?"

"What has she to do with that? Everything, as she has to do with all your thoughts, plans, and actions, and, sooth to say, with mine too! You want privately to send her a basket of game; you don't want old Ferret, or anyone else, to know anything about it; you want no hint of such lover-like and delicate attentions given to our father; and so you steal out like a poacher, and fill your bag on the sly."

"And you?"

"I the same. You know that I love Clarissa, and that till you came home—you, the heir, the future earl, the elder brother—I had reason to believe she liked me."

"No! no! no! thrice no!" cried the young lord; "Clarissa, from our earliest boyhood, preferred me."

"Ah! so your insolent vanity makes you imagine. You fancy, because Fortune has given you many other advantages, that she will give you that too; but I tell you, while you are beating about the bush, and, I dare say, planning to make the attorney's daughter—our mother's hired companion, the low-born Croft girl—your wife, I will steal a march upon you; not that I, my fine fellow am such a sawney fool as to meditate that greatest of mistakes, an unequal match; but-——"

"You dare not meditate anything against the honour of one who was as a daughter to our mother," cried the young lord, fiercely.

"Ha! ha! ha!" laughed the tempter; "and why not?"

Lord Hauteville's blood was on fire; he forgot himself; with the back of his hand he struck his brother across the face.

The next moment he felt ashamed of the indignity he had offered to one of his own proud race.

Wilfred stood before him, livid with rage,

for a moment paralysed with deadly revenge. There was foam on his white lip, and his every limb trembled.

"Brother, forgive me!" cried Lord Hauteville. "Strike me across the face in return," and he held his cheek to his brother, "and let us forget and forgive." His tears gushed forth as he spoke. "I will tell you presently why you must cease to follow up Clarissa—why you must think of her with respect, and speak of her with tenderness, but never dream of love as connected with her."

"You will?—you will tell me why everything worth living for is to be yours? Why all are to bow and cringe before you, and to be 'hail fellow, and well met,' with me? Why you are to lord it on two thousand, and I on five hundred a-year? Why you are to strike me with impunity, as you would your hound? Why the woman I love is to be torn from my life to adorn yours? And I will tell you in return, that I hate, that I loathe, that I curse you!—yes, from the depths of a broken heart I curse you! And as for Clarissa, I will never give up the pursuit—never, never, never!"

"Yes, you will, now at once, and for ever, when I tell you, when I swear to you by the heaven above us, that she is mine! Come, brother, forgive me! Shake hands, and listen to me. My own Clarissa is——"

As the beloved name passed his lips, the spirit of the first murderer entered the breast of the younger brother.

"How oft the means to do ill deeds make ill deeds done!"

His gun was loaded and cocked. In the fiend-like rage, envy, jealousy, and revenge of his heart, he took aim at the noble, beloved, and beautiful young form before him. Lord Hauteville, with a wild cry, sprang up with a bound, and then fell, in a huddled mass, on the ground, while, from the wound in his breast, the crimson blood welled forth, and a little rill from that red life-spring, his brother's heart, came trickling rapidly down to Wilfred's cold feet. The ground on which Lord Hauteville stood, when the fatal shot was fired, was rising ground; and down, down, quickly down, as if in pursuit of the fratricide, came the red life-blood, and Wilfred rushed from the spot with horror. He felt as if that blood would engulf his very soul. Yes, it was done! But was he a murderer? Life might not be quite extinct.

"No eyes have seen, no ears have heard what passed between us!" he said to himself. He thought he could hasten home through the fields, pretend to be about to summon Ferret and his son, and be by Hauteville's side in time to succour him if life were not extinct, and so divert all suspicion from himself if he were indeed dead.

All happened as he had expected. He gained the courtyard of the castle unseen, leaped into his own room at the open window, called Ferret and Joe, his son, the stopper, and saying he wanted to get a brace of pheasants for a friend, he led the way to the Black Wood, as it was called.

Altogether about an hour had elapsed since he had left that spot, with the brand of Cain upon his brow, and the curse of Cain on his life, and on his heart. Twice as he approached the dreadful spot a pheasant rose; twice he took aim, and twice he missed his aim; and old Ferret and his Joe marvelled, for Wilfred was what they called "a nailing shot," and seldom missed. At length they reached the little amphitheatre of grass, surrounded by yews, hollies, and ilex-trees.

Wilfred's knees shook; his heart seemed to die in his breast.

"Whatever ails Dido?" said old Ferret;

"what's she snuffing so hard at? Lord have mercy upon us! Whatever has been up here? The ground's all stained with blood! Oh! there's been murder done here!"

"My brother!" gasped Wilfred's conscience against his will. He did not dare to glance where he knew he had left his brother.

"Ay, Mr. Wilfred, it's my lord's gun a-lying here, sure enough; but how it came here, or whose blood's been shed, who's to guess?"

Wilfred, at these words, slowly and nervously turned his head. There was the blood-stained spot; the long grass, bent and clotted with gore, where his brother had fallen; but, alive or dead, the form of his brother was no longer there!

Wilfred was not imaginative—he was not superstitious.

"Some poachers have murdered him," he

gasped out, "and removed the body. Let us see if we can track their steps by the drops of blood."

Yes, that terrible track was to be seen, from the spot where Lord Hauteville had fallen, along the path through the wood, across the fields, and to the entrance of the villa of old Croft, the agent. The iron gates were open, the terrible track was on the wide gravel path, and glared frightfully on the broad stone steps, which the tidy housemaid had carefully pipeclayed.

Wilfred Lorraine was not, at that time, a hardened villain. His heart was new to the sense of actual crime; and when the parish doctor came downstairs, and not seeing him, said to the gamekeeper, whom he recognised,

"This is a bad job, Ferret. It's all over—he's done for! But who's to break it to the Earl and his brother?"

Wilfred's consciousness forsook him, and

he fell insensible on the floor. When he came to himself he was lying on the sofa in Mr. Croft's dining-room; the doctor was by his side, and Mr. Croft stood at a little distance, his arms folded, and eyeing him with an expression before which Wilfred cowered.

"Would *your Lordship*," said Mr. Croft, with a curious emphasis on the word, "like to go upstairs and see——"

"*Your Lordship!*" The once envied title sounded like a knell. He had not thought of the fact, that his brother's death made him Lord Hauteville, heir to the earldom—the future Lord Rockalpine. Bitterly as he had grudged his brother those titles, it was not for their sake he had done that dreadful deed —it was done in the wild height of those bad passions which had long smouldered in his breast, and which the blow he had received, and the announcement that Clarissa was his brother's, had wrought to the highest. But, oh! the vain remorse—the deep and shuddering chill! No coronet could remove the brand of Cain from his brow; no star, no ermine, could lighten his breast of its secret load of crime and anguish.

It seemed that some labourers, returning from their day's work, and thinking what a fine thing it would be to be a young lord, like the heir of Rockalpine, and to have no work to do but to shoot at will over those preserves, where, if they brought down a bird, or shot a hare, they would be punished as poachers, came suddenly on the object of their envy, bleeding to death in the wood, and his dog whining and howling as he watched by his master's side.

They at once suspected that he had been killed in an affray with some desperate poachers who infested the estate, and the name of Rough Rob passed from lip to lip.

While they were disputing what to do, Mr. Croft came up, and directed them to get a hurdle from the nearest fence, and to carry the victim to his house, which was much nearer and more accessible than the castle.

When Lord Hauteville was laid on the bed, and some restoratives had been administered, he rallied a little. Mr. Croft was alone with him, while the men went, some in search of the doctor, others to fetch a clergyman, and to break the terrible news to the Earl.

When the parson and the doctor came, he was breathing his last, and to the questions they put as to who had done the deed, he either could not or would not return any answer.

There was no evidence that he had spoken since he had received his death-wound.

The Earl bore his loss better than could have been expected. He had still an heir left; that heir was his favourite son.

A coroner's inquest sat upon the body—that beautiful and noble body! so lately warm with health and youth, and now cold clay. Many circumstances conspired to throw suspicion on Rough Rob.

Rough Rob's father, also a desperate poacher, had been killed in an affray with an under-gamekeeper of Lord Hauteville's, and Rough Rob had been heard to swear he would have blood for blood. Meantime, he owed the young lord a grudge for seizing his gun and his dog. He could not satisfactorily account for himself at the time of the murder. And all these things coming out at the inquest, the verdict found by the jury, and proclaimed in a loud, triumphant voice by their foreman, was one of

"WILFUL MURDER"

against Robin Redpath, commonly called Rough Rob.

Rough Rob was hooted as he was carried

off to the nearest magistrate by three policemen, and the crowd that followed the fly in which he was driven would gladly have torn him limb from limb.

CHAPTER III.

"Why did she love him? Curious fool, be still!
Is human love the growth of human will?
To *her* he might be gentleness. BYRON.

ROUGH ROB stood in the dock, with a policeman by his side; and even through the bronze of his weather-beaten face, there was a pallor which all present attributed to conscious guilt. There was also a visible tremor throughout his frame, and a huskiness about his voice. He was not an ill-looking man exactly, but he had something of the down-skulking look of the habitual poacher.

His poor wife, with a babe at her breast, was in court, weeping bitterly; she had persuaded him to smooth his shaggy hair, and plaster it down with grease, and to wash his face. She thought his *wild* look would go against him with the magistrate. She was a beautiful, devoted young creature, passionately attached to him. He wore an old velveteen shooting-jacket, with large horn buttons, and, owing to his Mary's forethought, he looked much more respectable, but much less picturesque, than usual.

Rough Rob's examination elicited that, on the day of the murder, he *was* out on the sly with his gun, and a lurcher, which he said had followed him.

When warned that he was not obliged to criminate himself, but that his words would be used in evidence against him, he said, in a tone very meek and subdued for such a ruffian—

"My lord, or rather, your worship—I can't criminate myself, and nobody can't criminate I; I'm as innocent of this black deed as the unborn babe, or as your lordship, which I means your highness. Why, it seems but yesterday that my young lord, and Master Wilfred, and I (poor hunted cretur that is now), wor all lads together. Father wor an earth-stopper then, on the estate, and I kept birds; and I was always a dab at fishing and setting traps and lines, and rat-catching, and all manner. And when my young lord and Master Wilfred came home from Eton, the first person they axed for were Rough Rob; and they'd get up o' the dark mornings, unbeknown, and slip out, and go ratting along of I. I taught 'em to shoot. They shot with my old gun afore they wor trusted with one of their own: and I taught 'em to fish, and make their own flies! And though I may have spoke a bit threat'ning or so when my lord took away my gun and my dog—which he done because he wor told a pack of lies about me shooting the hen pheasants, and a-getting partridges out of season—I'd have laid down my life for him, and he know'd it, too!"

Here Rough Rob's voice was broken by sobs, and tears filled his eyes. He mopped them up with his knuckles, and added, "I can't deny I was out with my gun, my lord, for the cupboard was bare—wife with a baby a-sucking and crying at her empty breast, and I out of work; but 'tain't because a man 'ud shoot a hare or a rabbit for his fasting wife's supper, and he's got a little bit of the radikel principle, and holds that wild things is meant for all, poor and rich, that he'd murder one he'd knowed from a boy, and spent many a jolly day with—one who'd often been a good friend to him and his'n, and who would never have been no other, but for meddling, jealous mischief-makers. If my young lord's spirit's here among us, he knows I speaks the truth, and that Rough Rob, so far from taking his precious life, would have shed his heart's blood to save him. That's all I've got to say, my lord. I'm a poor hunted cretur, but there isn't a man here more innocent of this crime, nor more cut up about it, than I be."

Rough Rob's earnest and agitated face formed a curious contrast to the bland, incredulous, and jauntily official air of the policeman by his side.

The magistrate, unluckily, knew Rough Rob's face too well. Twice indeed he had been brought before him.

The magistrate had a fine estate, preserved rigidly; and so far from thinking the game laws too stringent, thought them too lenient by far. A poacher, in his opinion, was capable of any amount of crime. Rough Rob had owned that he *was* out in the dark wood with his gun at the very time of the murder. He had owned he had used threatening words, and that he had owed Lord Hauteville a grudge for taking away his dog and his gun. There was no other person on whom a shadow of suspicion fell—no one else was out shooting in that wood at the time—no one else had felt or expressed any ill-will towards the young Lord, who was so deservedly popular, that, but for the vile grudge of one lawless man, he might have called him, in the words of the poet, "Good without effort, great without a foe."

The magistrate made one of his best speeches, for he knew the reporters were busy taking down every word he said; and no one present was at all surprised when, at the close of his long oration, he committed Rough Rob to prison to take his trial at the assizes for the wilful murder of Lord Hauteville. A piercing scream—a heart-rending scream—a wife's, a woman's scream—rang through the court as the magistrate pronounced this sentence; and Rough Rob's pretty young wife, with her babe at her breast, fell in a dead swoon into the extended arms of some kind sympathising woman near her. One young and nursing mother took the poor babe from its mother's cold exhausted breast, and warmed and nurtered it in her own. They tended the poacher's wife as if they had been her sister.

How kind the poor always are to the afflicted, the distressed, the disgraced! And what a sublime lesson do they give the rich, who fly from the lost and ruined, like rats from a falling house or a sinking ship!

Rough Rob was at once removed to the County Jail, and the hissings and hootings, and the execration of the mob (which had followed him to the police court), assailed him as he left it.

Alas for Rough Rob and his pretty young wife, just recovering to a sense of her misery!

The day of his brother's funeral was a terrible one for the fratricide.

On the plea of illness, both the proud old Earl and Wilfred, Lord Hauteville, had kept aloof as much as possible during the investigations and proceedings, but they could not absent themselves from the funeral.

Rough Rob, on his wretched pallet in Morpeth Jail, innocent of the crime for which he was now committed, was in a state of bliss, of beatitude, compared to the fratricide on the bed of down, that to him seemed full of thorns, when waked from hideous nightmares by the toll of the funeral bell booming on his ear.

He rose and dressed himself hastily, nervously, for the apartment seemed to him full of shades that took his murdered brother's form.

How tedious, how dreadful, were the preparations! How gravely officious were the undertaker and his assistants with the hatbands, scarfs, and gloves!

How horrible the whispers among the guests! for guilt is always afraid of a whisper.

How sickening the smell of all the gloves, hatbands, scarfs, and, above all, the funeral cake and wine! The long drive in a mourning-coach was maddening; slow, slow, slow, was the well-trained horses' pace, for they followed the hearse. What a black forest of plumes! How the dark, glossy feathers waved in the sunny breeze, sporting above the still and solitary inmate! A great crowd followed the funeral procession. The deceased had been so popular—the murder had caused so intense an excitement.

The church and the churchyard were soon filled, so were the lanes leading to it. All the well-to-do were in decent mourning. Even the poorest had rummaged up some bit of crape, brown with time, or an old faded black ribbon. The poor, though no hatbands, scarfs, or gloves were allotted them, were *chief mourners* at the young lord's funeral; he had been their best friend! The fratricide's fiercest trial was in the church, as he glanced at the coffin on the tressels, covered by the pall, and thought what it contained, and how it had come to pass; he could scarcely suppress a shriek, but an instinct of self-preservation prevailed, he went through it all with outward decorum, in spite of the hell within! It was over; the young lord was in the family vault—

"And dust to dust was given!"

The crowd dispersed, and the black coach bore the proud old Earl and his son back to the Castle.

The dreadful day was over, and night came at last! The moon was at her full, and her fair round face was mirrored in the large deep pools, and on the crystal shallows of the trout-stream that flowed through the Rockalpine estate. The pine-tree tops in the Black Wood were tipped with silver by her regal bounty, and the wild moors beyond were flooded by her radiance, and seemed almost as bright as by day.

With his hat drawn down over his brows, and an ample cloak concealing his form, Wilfred, Lord Hauteville, glided through that wood on his way to the lone hovel on the moor, once the wretched abode of Rough Rob, and still inhabited by his wife.

Oh! who that knows by his own experience, or will learn from that of others, what terror, anguish, and self-loathing attend on crime—who would not guard his heart from one sinful thought, and his hand from one act of guilt? A week ago, before "the deed that damns eternally was done," Wilfred Lorraine and his brother had gone out at night, by different roads, in search of poachers, and had agreed to meet at a certain old grand fir-tree in that wood!

Then Wilfred had no fear—for then he had

committed no crime. The half-moon shone then on a blooming, handsome, resolute face, a fine manly form, a firm foot. Now, the full moon looks on livid cheeks, eyes seared and hollowed, a figure shrunk and shrouded, a quick, uncertain step. In every breath of the night wind he hears his brother's sigh; every noise startles him; every ebon shadow cast by the silver lamp of night takes his brother's form; and the flitting of a white owl from tree to tree seems to him his brother's ghost coming out of the little grassy amphitheatre where he fell, to summon him to follow him to the grave. The Innocent, however hapless, go through a long life, without knowing a tithe of the anguish Hauteville felt in that midnight walk to Rough Rob's hut on the moor. He wildly rushed past the trees that enclosed the scene of the murder, and did not stop till he came out upon the purple moor.

He felt a little less of abject terror on the

moor than he had done in the Black Wood, but still there came cold drops on his forehead; his knees shook under him; and he had a horrible sense of being pursued.

He hurried across the wild moonlit moor, and at length came in view of Rough Rob's hovel. It was a wretched little cottage of clay, standing in a patch of potato and cabbage ground, and a gnome-like old thorn and a few furze-bushes close to it. As in all cottages in Northumberland, where coals are so cheap and abundant, a mound of coal-dust and ashes adjoined the house, and a shed full of coal formed part of the hovel.

There was a light in the small window, and through a broken pane came a voice of wild and exquisite sweetness, singing a sort of lullaby.

Hauteville listened. The air was changed to the old nursery ditty—originally the lullaby of a poacher's wife :—

"Bye, Baby Bunting,
Daddy's gone a-hunting,
Gone to find a pussy's skin
To wrap his precious baby in.
Bye, Baby Bunting!"

"Och hone! och hone!" sobbed the singer. "Och hone! that it were thrue, my darlint, then we'd have him soon back wid us—but now! Och hone! och hone! Holy Virgin protect my puir Rob! I've lighted a candle till ye; and to you, good Saint Robert, my puir Rob's pathron saint! And so I will, though I can ill afford it, for a month to come, if ye'll bring him safe back to me. Och hone! och hone!"

Lord Hauteville pushed open the cottage door, and stood in the only room it boasted. The young wife had just risen from her knees, and stood with a candle in her hand, which she had lighted in true Irish fashion, by thrusting it between the bars, and was just going to fix it in a little tin shrine, in which Saint Robert was placed.

The candle threw a strong light on Rob's wife. She was a beautiful young Irish girl, of that type which the inspired pencil of Edmund Fitzpatrick has immortalised. She was one of that influx of Irish reapers who, in the harvest season, come over to the North of England and fill the golden corn-fields with beauty, mirth, and song. Hauteville thought, as she stood before him, that she only wanted a wheat-sheaf on her head to be the *beau-ideal* of a Ruth, only that there was more of the wild daring of a daughter of Erin than of the meek sweetness of the young Hebrew widow. She was tall, and though she had the strong broad shoulders (mercifully given to the poor, who have so much to bear), yet they had a graceful fall, and her waist "fine by degrees and beautifully less," was marked by a scarlet bodice, while her short blue serge skirt showed her fine leg and neat foot and ankle, in red stockings and buckled shoes. A yellow handkerchief crossed her full and lovely bosom. Her head was proudly set on a long round sun-burnt throat; her abundant black hair, gathered under a Pamela cap, was braided in pretty ripples across a fine brow, and formed a soft frame to a face of great beauty; large, wild blue eyes, with long black lashes and jet eyebrows, a pretty straight nose, a short upper lip of soft red, the under one fuller, and of a brighter scarlet, and both, when she spoke, disclosing white, even, and glittering teeth. The baby, a fine little fellow, lay in the cradle covered with hare-skins, which she had stitched together.

The fire burned brightly, but the cupboard was bare, and Mary had tasted nothing that day but a cup of tea and a cake forced upon her, after Rob was carried off to jail, by the young nursing mother who had taken charge of her baby when she fainted, and who had compelled her to rest awhile in her poor little lodging and eat a morsel, and share that panacea of the poor, "a cup o' tea."

Mary, when she perceived Lord Hauteville, dropped a very low curtsey, and wiping down a chair with her apron, said,

"Plase your honour to be sated; ye may rest ye in my Rob's poor cabin, my lord, for the blood of yer blissed brother is not on his hand or his sowl! He's bearing the shame and the punishment he never desarved!"

In spite of his passionate and persistent love for Clarissa, Wilfred, or rather Hauteville, had often been struck with the rare beauty of the wild Irishwoman of the moor, and at any other time he could not have refrained from telling the lonely unprotected beauty how splendid a creature he thought her, and from trying at least to lead her into the slippery paths of dalliance; but the consciousness of a great crime sat on the young man's heart, and crushed out all its lighter foibles and vanities.

Beauty was nothing to him now—Love saw nothing. He seemed capable but of two feelings—horror of his crime, and dread of its discovery.

He had resolved that Rough Rob should not be brought to trial; no, not if he beggared himself to prevent it. But this resolve did not spring from the horror of the thought of another's suffering for his crime; no, *that* had little weight in his determination. It arose from his dread of the searching, sifting cross-examination! The truth, always so great, so potent, so all-pervading and convincing, never seems so irresistible, so unconquerable, as to the guilty man, whose *all* depends on its suppression.

"Facts are stubborn things," he said to himself, "and if it be true that 'murder will out,' it is at Rough Rob's trial that some astute and wily counsel for the defence will elicit it."

At this thought the murderer shook as with the ague; but he resolved on his plan of action. He had but one way to avoid the dreadful trial of Rough Rob, and that was, to effect Rob's escape from prison; and as it is not easy to escape from prison in these days, although such things have happened, and that recently, the young lord resolved to try bribery. Yes, he would bribe the jailer, whom he knew a little, for he had been in the Earl's service, and had been appointed at the entreaty of Wilfred.

Before going to Rough Rob's cottage on the moor, Wilfred had seen the jailer, and all was arranged between them. He had explained his wish to save Rough Rob, by the fact that he was the chosen companion in boyhood of himself and his murdered brother; and that, in spite of appearances, he believed him innocent, but yet he felt sure he would be found guilty and hanged.

Wilfred, Lord Hauteville, had to bribe very high, for the jailer felt he might lose his appointment; but no matter at what price, he must be bought over, and he was not to assist or co-operate, but to be blind and deaf.

Rough Rob must be communicated with, and put in the way of making his escape; but he was no scholar, he could not read writing; and so Wilfred resolved to let Rough Rob's wife into the secret, and to instruct her how, in an interview with her husband, to put him in the way of escaping, and joining her and their infant at a wild rocky creek, where a boat was to be in readiness to row them to B——, whence an Australian ship was about to sail for the Land of Promise.

Wilfred had to find them funds, and to pay

for their passage; but he felt that Rob's escape would confirm the impression of his guilt, and that Rob once safe off, he should breathe more freely.

"What would yer honour plase to want wid me?" said Mary.

"I want to know whether, if, for the sake of old times, I could manage that Rob should escape from jail, you would be willing to go to Australia with him?"

"Would I? Oh, yer honour, wouldn't I go wid Rob wherever God and he plases? But why need he escape? He's innocent as his babe in the cradle there; and why would he flee like a guilty cratur?"

"Because, guilty or not guilty, he's sure to be condemned—circumstantial evidence is so strong against him. Well, as I said before, for the sake of old times, and the love my poor brother once had for Rob, I'll contrive an opportunity for you to see him, and to tell him to loosen a bar of his window. You'll give him this book to wile away the time. It is called 'The Prisoner's Help and Guide;" and so it is, in sooth, for look, in the back is a caseful of tools—you touch this spring, so, and then they appear. Well, tell him to tie his bed-clothes together, and let himself down from the window on the leads, in the dead of to-morrow night, and then to make for the creek, where he will find you, your babe, and the boat awaiting him."

"Oh! yer honour," said Mary, "how will I ever thank yer? But will not my poor Rob be overheard and stopped?"

"No; I've managed all that."

"The Saints and the Blissed Virgin reward yer as yer deserves!" said Nora.

Wilfred winced and shuddered.

"I understand, it's gold is the key as will let my Rob out. And is there no oder hope? If they will find him guilty that's innocent of all but shooting wild things, which, we both thinks, He, who cares for the Poor and feeds the ravens, sint more for them, than for the Rich; for haven't you yer capons and yer ducks, and yer noble jints, and hot soups, and sweets, and we almost dying of hunger, agra? Very true, it's against the law; and Rob's being a poacher will set all the judges against him."

"He has no other chance; will you do what I have explained to you?"

"Och hone! och hone!" cried the poor wife. "I'm sorely tempted; but what's to become of his good name?"

Wilfred could not suppress a ghastly smile at the thought of the good name of Rough Rob, the notorions poacher.

"Och hone!" she cried, glancing mournfully at the babe in the cradle. "Maybe, if I consint, the day'll come when they'll up and tell thee, my darlint, that thy dad was a murtherer—a base dog, that bit the hand that had often fed and stroked him. And my friends, masther—my lord, I mane—they were dead agin the match; for though I came over here a poor raper, my great-grandmother, on mother's side, rode in her coach and four; and the blood of the O'Rourkes, that's fader's side, once flowed in the veins of an ould Irish king, and now to come to this! Och hone! och hone!" she cried, wringing her hands; "if I could but see Father Mahoney, he'd advise wid me for the best!"

"You shrink from it, then? You will let Rob stand his trial. Remember, I warn you, he will be found guilty, and hanged by the neck till he is dead! dead! dead!"

"Oh! no, no! It's not that, your honour," cried the wife, wringing her hands, tearing her long black hair, and beating her lovely bosom. "No, no, no, my lord! do not spake them terrible words; on my sowl I cannot bear them!"

"How will you bear the reality, if yo cannot endure the idea, woman?"

"I'll go till him; I'll take him the buke and show him the tules. I'll pray to him, for my sake, for our baby's sake; and yet I may not be acting like a loyal, honest wife, for I know him innicent, and yet would have him stale away like a guilty, blude-stained wretch. What will I do! what will I do!"

It ended, of course, in her agreeing to help to promote Rough Rob's escape. And Wilfred went back to the castle, taking a very long, circuitous route, to avoid crossing the Black Wood again.

Two days later, the papers were full of Rough Rob's daring and clever escape from M—— jail.

There was great excitement, and great discontent and disappointment about it, and the police were active in pursuit; but no trace was discovered of him, or his wife and child. In fact, it was not till he had been gone twelve hours that the jailer gave the alarm.

Mary's Irish eloquence had prevailed; Rough Rob had agreed to avail himself of the means of escape; and while the police were hunting woods, and groves, and rocks, and chalkpits, little town rooms and country hovels, Rough Rob, with his wife and child, were sailing across the broad Pacific. And Rough Rob's heart was light, for he was innocent; and as they were all the world to each other as long as they were together, he and his Mary cared not whither they went.

But even he could not bear to leave a murderer's name behind, and he made his Mary seek out Lord Hauteville, and exact a promise from him to leave no stone unturned to discover the real murderer, and to do his best to clear, from so black a blot, the name of Rough Rob.

CHAPTER IV.

> "So, for a good old gentlemanly vice,
> I think I shall take up with avarice."
>
> BYRON.

THE escape of Rough Rob left no doubt of his guilt on the mind of any one. It was evident he dared not face the mass of evidence that would be brought against him.

His crafty and daring escape was a nine days' wonder, and then other events occurred to excite and occupy public attention, and Rough Rob sank into comparative oblivion.

Nearly a year had passed, and Wilfred, Lord Hauteville, had hoped that when Rough Rob was far away, and the perils of the trial were averted, he should be able to sleep and rest. Alas! like Macbeth, he had "murdered sleep," and driven rest from his life and soul.

The old Earl had always lived in comparative solitude. He was a lonely being, and had but one passion, almost always cultivated in solitude—Avarice. To hoard was his great delight; the chink of the ruddy gold was the only sound he loved to hear; money-bags and iron chests were his chosen companions.

This vice, for surely it is a vice, and a very mean one, like Aaron's rod, swallowed up all others.

As a young man he had been proud, vain, and a great worshipper of beauty, as his marriage proved. He had been ambitious. Now he was nothing but a miser. And he spent as much time, and used as many arts to conceal his hoards and to tell them over, as if the glittering piles were not his own by right, but stolen from others. He had no interest in his son, or in anything but his gold.

And Lord Hauteville's loneliness had become so odious and intolerable—for a bad conscience is a guest never so unendurable as in solitude—that he resolved to marry; to marry some heiress, who would rejoice to barter her wealth for a title and a future coronet, and with whom he could live in the gay world, whose noise, tumult, and din would, he hoped, drown the "still small voice."

There was a lady of fabulous wealth, on whom Wilfred had long cast an eye. She belonged to his own county, and lived in a new but gorgeous hall, some fifteen miles from Rockalpine Castle. Her father was one of the greatest of our princely coal-masters. He was a self-made man; and was M.P. for the northern division of his native county.

Sir James Armstrong was a very fine, manly fellow; but Miss Armstrong, though pretty and accomplished, was, at heart, vulgar, ambitious, and ashamed of her poor relations and low origin, and resolved to obtain that unquestionable rank and position which a grand marriage alone would ensure. She had always intended to be married to *Lord Hauteville;* and though he at whom she had aimed was in his grave, yet a *Lord Hauteville* was still to be had, and she resolved to have him. Worldly as she was, she was only seventeen, and singularly elegant and pretty.

Lord Hauteville, having ascertained that Pride had been so completely swamped by Avarice in his father's breast that he was willing to receive the low-born heiress as a daughter-in-law, resolved to wait on the young lady.

He determined to ride over to Armstrong Hall, quietly and unattended. He had now a great dread, a vague but terrible dread, of servants' gossip, and so he would not take a groom. He was too great, and his position too lofty and too well understood, for *him* to care, like a meaner suitor, for pomp or display. No; he would ride over and see the young lady, and, if she welcomed him, he would make very short work of it, and get her to name the day.

It was a glorious morning in August. The sun shone as it does in Italy. Its intense brilliancy created a solitude on the moors. Grouse shooting had not yet commenced, and the forests and the woods were cool and pleasant in comparison.

Lord Hauteville rode over to Armstrong Hall. He was kept some time waiting before the young lady appeared. She was making an elaborate toilet. At length she appeared, over-dressed, but looking very pretty. She proposed to show Lord Hauteville a new annual in her own parterre. She culled for him a heart's-ease, very large and of a pale lilac, which was called the Annabella, after herself.

Wilfred held, for a moment, the fair little hand which, without a flutter, remained in his, saying,

"Will you make this heart's-ease an everlasting flower, by giving me the hand that offers it?"

The young lady replied,

"If papa consents, I agree."

And thus did the young lord propose, and thus did the young lady accept. They were both young, both beautiful—a blue sky above them, and flowers of every hue at their feet. But this world was too much with them—and their troth was plighted, without a blush on the part of the maiden, or a quickened pulse on that of the suitor.

Lord Hauteville left Armstrong Hall, and, remounting his pony, took his lonely way back to the castle.

As he recrossed the moor, just where it adjoined, on one side, the fields, with their circuitous bridle-road, and, on the other, the Black Wood, he overtook a tall, slight female form, which suddenly sprang up from behind a large furze-bush, and rushed wildly on towards the Black Wood. That form was very wasted, the dress was torn, soiled, uncared for; the long golden hair streamed over the shoulders; there was no hat, hood, or bonnet on the little Grecian head; but there was a wreath of wild-flowers—poppies, corn, and grass, an Ophelia wreath—round the pale brow.

Lord Hauteville grew ghastly pale. He felt, though he did not see the face, and though the once rounded form was so wasted—he felt he gazed on Clarissa!

He had heard nothing, seen nothing, of that hapless girl since his brother's death.

He had not dared to seek her, or inquire after her.

He dreaded her anguish, her despair. And there she was, and—oh! horror of horrors!—the sun's rays flamed on something she held in her hand. It was a knife!

Instinctively Lord Hauteville followed her.

On, on she sped; passing unheeded the water, across the shallow brook, she entered the dark wood, and instinctively he followed her. He leaped from his pony, tied him to a tree, and hurried after Clarissa.

Angel of Death! she has stopped where the evergreens fence in the little grassy amphitheatre. Alas! it had been a trysting-place of love!

"She has heard that he died there," said Wilfred to himself, "and there she means to kill herself."

And, at the thought, he darted forward,

and, just as she knelt on the spot where *he* had fallen, the fratricide stole behind her, and snatched the upraised knife from her hand.

"Ha, ha! is it you?" shrieked Clarissa, the fire of madness in her eyes. "And you will not let me join him? Hist, hist! do you not know he was mine? Mine through time and through eternity! Ha, ha, ha! I saw it all in a dream. Murderer!—Fratricide! —you have killed my darling!"

"Hush, hush!" said Lord Hauteville, "you are mad! you rave! Let me take you home to your father's house. Are you staying there? Have you escaped? Where would you go?"

"To him! to him! to him!" shrieked the maniac, tearing up the grass, and struggling to get free, and to repossess herself of the knife.

Just at this moment Lord Hauteville heard

the voices of Ferret, Joe, and the head groom. He called to them; they came and helped him to bind the poor crazy Clarissa, and to convey her to her father's villa.

Her escape had just been discovered; she had been at home only a few days, and her stepmother and her attendants were in search of her. Mr. Croft was from home. He was gone in search of some asylum where she could be placed in safety, for her malady had been increased by her return to her home.

Mrs. Croft was young and pretty, but a very artful, time-serving, hard woman; she expressed the greatest gratitude to Lord Hauteville, who fully impressed upon her that Clarissa Croft ought to he placed in a private lunatic asylum, as her mind was completely gone. He then took his way home, and the echo of Clarissa's shrieks long rung in his ears.

By degrees she became calm, and so rational that she was allowed to return to the charge of that kind aunt who had been as a mother to her. Here her malady took the form of a settled melancholy, varied by occasional affecting intervals of half-crazy, half-frantic mirth. Here, too, she was allowed the solace of the company of her child —a child born in secrecy, a noble little fellow, about three years of age.

Her chief amusement was to twine bridal wreaths and bouquets, and throw a long muslin scarf over her head like a veil, and then, with a garland on her forehead, she would kneel before a couch, as if it were an altar, and place a chaplet on the head of her child, and call him her Hauteville.

One day she was thus engaged in the room appropriated to her—(her aunt was living in a suburb of London, and Clarissa's expenses were defrayed by her father)—when that father, accompanied by his young wife, arrived at her aunt's. Mrs. Miller was not at home, but Mr. Croft at once proceeded to the room where Clarissa was.

As he opened the door, his sly, smiling wife by his side, a spasm contracted his heart and brow.

There was that wreck of beauty, talent, love!

There was Clarissa—poor, crazy Clarissa—veiled, wreathed, kneeling before a couch, which she called the altar, and crowning with flowers the head of the little child, whom she addressed as her "Hauteville." Young Mrs. Croft persuaded her old husband that a private lunatic asylum was the only fit place for the maniac, and that it was very dangerous to trust the child with a crazy mother.

Clarissa, upon this, was removed to a private mad-house, called "The Happy Home," and Mr. Croft took charge of the little boy.

The parting from her child was the overflowing drop in Clarissa's cup of bitters. She did not survive her removal to "The Happy Home" more than a month.

The same day that saw Clarissa laid in her quiet grave at K—— Cemetery, saw Lord Hauteville united to Annabella, only child of Sir James Armstrong, Bart., M.P., of Armstrong Park, and the old Earl chuckling over this addition to the family wealth.

CHAPTER V.

"If thou wilt marry, I will give thee this plague for thy dowry—
Be thou as cold as ice, as pure as unsunned snow,
Thou shalt not escape calumny."

HAMLET.

THERE was a good deal of whispering among the old maids at A—— (the country town nearest to Rockalpine), and scraggy necks were stretched, and quaint old heads met over the tea-tables, and eyes were cast up and mouths were drawn down; and all this was because Mr. Croft had brought back with him to Croft Villa a beautiful little boy of three years old, whom he called his grandson. This child was in deep mourning, as indeed were Mr. and Mrs. Croft.

The child was named Arthur Bertram, and was introduced as an orphan.

Mr. Croft merely gave out that his daughter Clarissa, while in London, had made an imprudent love-match with a young man called Bertram, who had died suddenly, after they had been four years secretly married; that she had concealed her marriage from fear of the anger of her father and her other friends, but had confided it to her too indulgent aunt; that Clarissa had taken her husband's death so much to heart, that she had been attacked by brain fever, and had fallen a victim to that dreadful malady, leaving behind her one child, this boy, whom he (with Mrs. Croft's sanction) had adopted, and intended to bring up with his own young family.

The second Mrs. Croft had already presented her lord with five pledges of her affection, the eldest of whom was an ugly, unamiable boy of six, when little Arthur was introduced at Croft Villa.

It was about Arthur and his poor mother, the once beautiful and envied Clarissa Croft, that the old maids at A—— were so bitter and so busy. They had formed their own opinions of the parentage of little Arthur. They disbelieved the whole story of the clandestine marriage, and had no faith in the late Mr. Bertram. They said, with a sort of triumph, that they had always prophesied that Lawyer Croft would have good cause to repent letting his daughter be brought up with two young noblemen; and that all had turned out exactly as they had foretold. They considered young Mrs. Croft a great fool for allowing the child to be domesticated with her own; and they thought it was a sin and a shame, as matters had turned out (and as his father had been cut off in his sins, and had made no provision for the little unfortunate wretch), that he was not sent at once to some orphan asylum.

Meanwhile, the Earl of Eaglescliffe had grown older, greyer, balder, and colder—more stern, more selfish, and more avaricious than ever. He lived entirely at Rockalpine Castle; and as counting his hoards was his only amusement, occupation, and excitement, and he was exposed to no dangers, no changes of atmosphere, and no risks of any kind, there seemed to be no reason why he should not live on to an extreme old age. Lord Hauteville's marriage with the only child and heiress of Sir James Armstrong had rendered him in a great degree independent of his father's wealth; but as heir to the earldom, he had the two thousand per annum which his murdered brother had enjoyed, and an estate of considerable value, which his father's mother had entailed on the eldest surviving son of the house of Rockalpine, and which was to be his absolutely on his attaining the age of twenty-five. This estate, which was called Beech Park, was in Berkshire, close to Windsor Forest, and it in due time became the country seat of Lord and Lady Hauteville.

Lord Hauteville was, of course, in his inner self, a miserable man, for the consciousness of guilt sat heavy on his soul, and the possibility of detection often palsied him with fear. But he tried to lose the memory of the Past in political excitement. He entered Parliament, he studied oratory, and became a popular speaker. He applied himself to finance, and became useful to his party. He set charities on foot, promoted the building of schools and reformatories, and the amelioration of prison discipline. His name headed every subscription for the good of the masses. He had a morbid craving for that popular esteem, which he well knew he had forfeited; and he worked incessantly to obtain present power and popularity, and to drown thoughts of the future and the past.

In his own family, he was cold, stern, reserved; but he let Lady Hauteville have her own way, and allowed her to spend as she pleased a considerable portion of the income she had brought him.

There was no affection, no sympathy, between them; but then, *à fortiori*, there was none of the jealousy of love, none of its dissensions. Whatever other noblemen (who stood high as husbands and fathers) did by their wives and children, he did; and the world quoted him as a moral man, a religious man, a good husband, and a model father!

"Wise judges are we of each other!" The world little dreamt that the hand so ready with the annual subscription or the large donation was red with a brother's blood; or that the great reformer, who was so anxious about the moral improvement and sanitary condition of our prisons, ought to be himself a prisoner in Newgate, and to cross its threshold only for the scaffold.

Time rolled on; Lord Hauteville stood very high both with the few in power, and with the many to whom they owe that power. He had been for some time member for Rockalpine, when the death of one of the county members gave him an opportunity of offering himself as a candidate for nomination as one of the M.P.'s for North N——. His politics and principles were of the popular kind (then in the ascendant). His family influence was very great; the Rockalpine property was very large; but the election was fiercely contested by two other candidates, of even greater family wealth and influence; and yet Lord Hauteville was returned. His reputation carried it!

So good, so gifted, so useful! A man not merely of such virtuous and noble thoughts and principles, but a man of action, too! A moral man, a pious man, a good churchman. Not a gay man; there were no sad stories afloat about *him*. It was a fierce contest, and a great triumph, and it was followed by a greater still.

A change in the ministry caused three important vacancies. One of them was offered to Lord Hauteville. He had always longed for office—not merely on account of the power it gave him, but for the sake of the absorbing occupation it ensured, the engrossing labour it compelled. These promised a safe and constant refuge from thought.

Of course, previous to his accepting the office, he had to resign his seat, and to be re-elected. He did not feel quite safe and secure of re-election; for not only a guilty conscience made him afraid of everything and everybody, but he had received several anonymous letters, written in a mysterious, a menacing, and to him a very startling tone; warning him that he had a secret foe, and that he had better not carry his head so high, nor look down on better men than himself; that he was *not born to be drowned*, and was better known than he imagined.

To any man of Lord Hauteville's position, blest with "the princely heart of innocence," these anonymous attacks would have appeared as the result of private or politic pique, and he would either have burnt them at once, or have put them into the hands of a detective.

But not so Lord Hauteville. They drove the blood from his cheek, they shook him as the ague might have done. They made his flesh creep, his knees knock together, his head swim, and his heart sink.

They might mean nothing; they were couched in the ordinary cant of those meanest of the weapons of vulgar, coward, and vile enmity—anonymous letters. The words "*not born to be drowned*" would have made an innocent man of Lord Hauteville's rank, station, and reputation laugh; but to *him*, the murderer, the fratricide, who knew in his secret heart that he *deserved* to be *hanged*, those words made him feel as if a rope were tightening itself round his throat.

However, after the first servile palsy of fear, he roused himself. He thrust the letters into the fire; and hearing that Lady Hauteville was still asleep (she had been up late at a ball the night before), he set off for Cumber-court (where he was expected), resolved to do his utmost to ensure his re-election; for of course on that re-election his being in office depended. Mr. Croft, his father's agent and lawyer, had a good deal to do with the election; and as Lord Hauteville had a nervous horror of Croft Villa, he sent for Mr. Croft to the Castle.

Mr. Croft in his heart owed Lord Hauteville

many a bitter grudge. Mr. Croft was a man of very humble origin, and was mean enough to be ashamed of what ought to have been his pride and glory, namely, that he was a self-made man. He had been a charity or blue-coat boy at N——; and when Hauteville was a younger son, and very haughty, insolent, and overbearing, he once forgot himself so far as to remind Mr. Croft of his origin, and that in presence of several strangers. This he did in revenge for Mr. Croft's complaining to the Earl of the young gentleman's breaking his fences, and treading down his corn.

Mr. Croft was not a noble-hearted man. He never forgave the boyish affront.

However, it was now Lord Hauteville's policy to conciliate Mr. Croft, and Mr. Croft *appeared* to be conciliated. He was always rather stiff and cold certainly; but he professed to be at his lordship's service, while in heart he was as bitter as ever.

On his arrival at Rockalpine, Lord Hauteville, as usual, waited on the old Earl, who, disturbed in counting over some gold, which he hastily thrust into a drawer, paid little attention to his son's plans and projects. While the son was sitting (as a mere form) opposite to his father, Mr. Croft was announced. Lord Hauteville soon arranged matters with him, and the lawyer took his leave. Lord Hauteville then strolled out.

It was a lovely spring day, or rather evening, and Lord Hauteville walked briskly on, to look at the young plantations, and, as he rambled along some newly-made paths, unexpectedly to himself he came to the entrance of the Black Wood. By this time the shades of evening were closing in, and the Black Wood looked blacker than ever.

In spite of himself his eye *would* try to pierce those deep, mysterious shades; and the memory of the dreadful crime he had committed there, came back on his mind with the freshness of yesterday; when suddenly a tall, hooded female form in black advanced to the entrance opposite to which he stood, and beckoned him to follow her into the wood. Mechanically he obeyed. The "Woman in Black" led the way, until they reached the little grassy amphitheatre where the fratricide had slain his brother!

Lord Hauteville recoiled. The woman, who was a little in advance of him, turned back, approached him, seized him by the arm, and half persuaded, half compelled him to enter the little enclosure. She then threw back the hood that had concealed her face, and Lord Hauteville recognised Rough Rob's handsome Irish wife, Mary.

"I have bickoned you here, my lord," she said, "because we'll not be interrupted here. The people say the place is haunted, your honour; and they'il kip clear of it, anyhow."

"But what do you want with me, Mary?" said Lord Hauteville, sternly.

"Rob's wid me," she said.

"Where? and what of that?"

"He repints that he did not stand his thrial, yer honour. He's sure he'd have been acquitted, because he knows he's innicent. And we don't like Australy, noways. We've lost all our childrin; we can't rare a living child noways out there, yer honour; and it breaks our hearts to see 'em die, and to have to lay 'em in that unnat'ral soil, so far from home, where the flowers have no swate smill, nor the birds no song. We've thried now many a long year, and we're heart-sick wid it, and that's the blessed thruth! And we can't make both inds meet, noways. And you've been the friend in need till us, and so we're come to till you all, and consult wid yer honour. We've a good chance in Ameriky, where I've kith and kin; but we want a good lump of money, and then Rob could jine in partnership wid my cousin, Mike O'Rourke, and git on a bit, and pay yer honour the money we owes you, back agin when we've got smooth a bit, and aren't drove as we are now. Mike has got a tidy bit of money to invist, and has been unkimmin kind, and spent a sight in bringing us over here, and fitting Rob up dacent; but we tould him we'd a good grand friend, who'd help us, maybe, when he heerd the rights on it. And onst up in the world a little, Rob 'ud come over, and shtand his thrial like an innicent man as he is. And he says he'd have all the best lawyers and counsillors in England; and he's certain his innicence would be proved, and the guilty would be deticted."

Lord Hauteville winced, turned pale, and averted his eyes from Mary's flashing glance and animated face.

"If not, he's for giving himself up to be

thried at onst; and I've had hard work to hinder him. But I owns I remimbers yer honour's words, and I dreads the verdict, innicent as I knows Rob to be."

"Where is poor Rob?" said Lord Hauteville, tenderly, and as if he felt deeply for him.

"He's jist hiding up till dark, in the ould cabin on the moor. We found it as we lift it, yer honour. No one has ever thried to live there, because they think it was a murtherer's house, and that my young lord's sperit walks there! Well, Rob's hiding there; and he bade me (for I'd heard you were expicted the day) to be on the look-out to spake wid your honour, and to say, if you'll lave the library winder opin, as you used to do in the dear ould days, when you and my dear young murthered lord were lads, he'll come round at midnight to spake wid yer honour."

"Tell him I shall expect him, Mary," said

Lord Hauteville, putting some gold into her hot, trembling hand. "And bid him keep close, or they'll nab him; and if they do, innocent though he be, they'll hang him."

The wife turned deadly pale, and hurried off at these words, after dropping a very low rustic curtsey to his lordship, and calling on the Blessed Virgin and Rob's patron saint to reward him as he deserved; and Lord Hauteville, thrilled with horror to find himself standing on the very spot where his brother fell, slain by him, gazed around him with a glance of terror.

As he did so, the moon came out—the full moon—and lighted up the tree at whose base his brother had fallen. To his horror, he saw that the exact date of the murder was cut in the bark, and his murdered brother's initials, and his own also. They were picked out with red—that sort of raddle with which sheep are marked; and under his brother's monogram was a coffin, and under his own a coronet, while a little lower down, to his dismay, he saw a gallows deeply cut into the bark of the old tree, marked out in black, and the motto, "I BIDE MY TIME!" legibly chiselled above it.

Who had done all that? and what did it mean? Hauteville's heart beat high against his cold breast, as he sped, like one pursued, back to the Castle.

* * * * * *

At midnight, a tap at the library window (which he had left partly open) made him start. He hastened to see who was there, and—though looking older, sterner, stouter, and more respectable than of yore—he recognised Rough Rob. His sunburnt face was pressed against the glass of the window, which flattened his nose, and gave him a strange, ogre-ish, unnatural appearance.

The interview was not a pleasant one; for when Lord Hauteville, seeing Rough Rob almost decided on standing his trial, started from his chair with assumed fierceness, and called him a fool, a doomed, predestined, obstinate, pig-headed victim, Rough Rob answered angrily, and was about to leave the room, with the words—

"I may be a fool, my lord, and I may be a victim, but I'm not a murderer. And if I don't give myself up like an innocent man now, at onst, and stand my trial, I'll not die till I've done it. And I only gives in now because of Mary being so dead agen it, and a man standing so poor a chance if he've got no friend in his pocket to help him."

"Well," said Lord Hauteville, "Mary has told me of your plans, and, for the sake of old times, I'm willing to forward them. Name the sum you want, and you shall have it. But get out of this neighbourhood at once, or, as sure as you stand there, you'll be taken, tried, and hanged."

"I don't believe it, my lord," said Rob. "I believe my innocence would be made clear as the sun at noonday, and that the Guilty would be brought to justice. That's my belief; but I'll be ruled by you, my lord. Mary's cousin, Mike O'Rourke, he's fitted me up in these clothes. He's helped us back, and he's getting his matters settled to go to 'Meriky; and if I can get three hundred pound, he'll take me into partnership as a farmer."

"Here is the money," said Lord Hauteville, taking out his pocket-book; "and fifty more for your passage. But begone now, in Heaven's name, or you'll be taken, as sure as there's a God in Heaven! Stop! I'll see you safe on to the moor; or stay—I was going to drive over to Armstrong Hall. Go you and await me at the cross-road on the moor. I'll send my groom back on some pretext or another before I join you. We'll then take up Mary at the old hut, and I'll set you down within five minutes' walk of the station."

All was managed as the trembling, anxious culprit proposed; and Rob and his wife got safe off to London by the mail-train, joined Mike O'Rourke at his lodging in St. Giles's, and ultimately sailed for America, to the unspeakable relief of the real culprit.

CHAPTER VI.

"She will have just the life she prefers,
With little to wish or to fear;
And ours will be pleasant as hers,
Might we view her enjoying it here."

COWPER.

LADY HAUTEVILLE was intensely ambitious, vain, calculating, and worldly. Her marriage and her money gave her position and power. She longed to be a countess, and to sit, in her coronet and robes, in the House of Peers, on all grand occasions; and she grudged the old miser Earl, at Rockalpine, his protracted existence, and thought it a cruel dispensation that he should live on—on—on! But she resolved to make the most of the advantages she *had* ensured by her union with a peer's eldest son.

She was a *parvenue*, it is true; but she became popular. The fine ladies of Belgravia and Mayfair said, behind their fans, that "*parvenues* were so agreeable, because they were not exactly like other people;" by which they meant, like their august, high-bred, haughty selves. But Lady Hauteville could be haughty too, and often, by sheer impudence, she compelled them to court her. Lady Hauteville's dinners, "at homes," concerts, picnics, balls, and private theatricals were the rage.

She was pretty, clever, daring, and accomplished. She dressed to such perfection—(taking care to get all her things from the milliners and mantua-makers of Eugénie, Empress of the French)—that she set the fashions in England. She knew when to be grand and defiant, and when to be humble and conciliating.

She had a son and three daughters, born in

the early years of her marriage; and six years later, a fourth girl came into the world, unwelcome and unwished-for; somehow, her arrival interfered with some fashionable arrangements of her worldly mother's; and as she was rather a delicate, sickly child, and did not possess the regular beauty of her elder sisters, Lady Hauteville from the first treated her rather as an intruder, and took no interest whatever in her.

The pride (which she called maternal affection) with which she regarded her boy, her son, her heir (the future Earl of Rockalpine), and even her three elder girls—had no part in her feelings towards poor little Edith.

To add to this worldly mother's dislike, the poor little girl, left in her lonely, deserted, but once bustling, merry nursery, to the care of servants, met with an accident while the family were staying on an annual visit to the old Earl at Rockalpine.

The doctors decided that the spine was injured, and they announced, in conclave, that they much feared that Edith would be a cripple.

They said she must live entirely in the country, and not far from the sea, and must remain constantly in a reclining posture.

Edith, at this time, was eight years of age. Her three sisters were respectively eighteen, seventeen, and sixteen, and her brother fourteen. As Lady Hauteville had resolved that very spring to present her two elder daughters, Augusta and Georgina, she was not at all disposed to postpone a matter of such "importance"—in her opinion—for the sake of poor little Edith.

At the same time, she knew that Lord Hauteville would not risk the censure of the little world of Alnwick and Rockalpine by neglecting the Doctor's advice about the poor little invalid. However, diplomacy, and the spirit of manœuvering, came to her aid.

Two years before Edith's accident she had made a long stay at Rockalpine Castle (for the air of the north was considered bracing for Edith); and the old miser Lord, hearing that little Edith, who was his favourite, was ordered to spend the summer by the sea, had proposed, as a saving of expense, that she should stay with her nurse at the castle; and, in accordance with his wish, she had been left there for several months with one female attendant.

She had been much courted during her stay at Rockalpine by the Crofts; and the lonely child had felt very grateful for their kindness and attentions, and had found great delight in the company of the Croft children, and still more in that of Arthur Bertram.

During that long visit of Edith's, the old Earl had at first continued to live almost entirely in his own rooms, with no company but his money-bags; but little Edith, whose loving, pitying nature made her cling even to the stern, grey old man, would sometimes knock at his door with a basket of wild flowers, and coax him out for a walk in the sun, or the woods, or by the sea. And the cold, worldly, lonely old man grew fond of the only thing that sought and liked his company; and a sort of friendship grew up between these opposite natures.

Lord Hauteville, for some reason or other which he never explained, and perhaps could not have defined, was always very civil and conciliatory to Mr. Croft; and Lady Hauteville, in a visit she paid to Mrs. Croft, contrived so adroitly to blend her wish to leave Edith at Rockalpine, with the impossibility of sacrificing her eldest daughter's prospects, or of trusting the little invalid to a servant, that Mrs. Croft offered to take charge of the young lady, and to give her every possible advantage, and the greatest care and most attentive and tender nursing.

Mrs. Croft did not say a word about any pecuniary arrangement, as connected with this matter; but she was very fond of money, and had an eye to the main chance in the proposal she made. Mr. Croft, who was a most hen-pecked husband in every other respect, was still, as yet, sole and supreme master of his cheque-book and purse. And Mrs. Croft contrived so that whatever was paid for the board and lodging of Edith should be received by herself, so that she might be enabled to indulge in every expensive whim of her own eldest son, her idol and her pet, Roger.

Roger was at Eton; and while his father's object was to bring him up to the Church (Lawyer Croft had a living ready for him), Roger himself, and his fond mother, had other views. Roger wished to be a man of fashion, and to mix with noblemen; and even at Eton he tried hard to acquire the reputation of wealth and liberality.

Lord Hauteville was very well pleased when his lady told him of Mrs. Croft's proposal. He agreed to the payment of a handsome stipend for Edith's board and lodging; and though he never went to the Villa—for he had a great horror of the spot in which his brother had breathed his last, and of ascending those door steps which had been blotted with that brother's life-blood—he got the old Earl to consent to his inviting Mr. and Mrs. Croft to dinner at the Castle, for the purpose of completing the final arrangements about the abode of Edith at Croft Villa.

"Well, my dear Augusta," said Lady Hauteville to her eldest daughter, after Edith had been carried off in Mrs. Croft's brougham, to reside at Croft Villa for an indefinite period, "well, I'm very glad that's settled. It would, indeed, have been a sad thing if your presentation and Georgina's had been delayed on account of poor Edith; and yet, if Mrs. Croft had not so kindly offered to take her, what could have been done?"

"I suppose she must have remained here with grandpapa and her nurse, mamma," said Miss Augusta, very coldly. "It would have been too absurd to keep Georgina and me back on account of that little carroty cripple!"

"I think," said Miss Georgina, "much too great a fuss is made with Edith; a little, sickly, ugly thing!"

"She has not your beauty, certainly, my dears," said Lady Hauteville; "and, I own, I do not like her disposition or her manners. She has no dignity, no proper pride, no lady-like reserve, no necessary little feminine artifice; but I beg, my loves, you will not forget she is your sister, and an invalid, and that it is bad taste not at least to *appear* to feel an affectionate interest in her!"

Bad taste! It never struck Lady Hauteville that it was very bad feeling—that she cared little about.

But were the cold, proud young beauties right? Was Edith Lorraine "a carroty cripple," and a "sickly, ugly, little thing?" Her hair was certainly of a very red auburn, and ill-nature might call it carroty, but it was most silken, profuse, and rippled; and was just of the hue to ripen into the colour of the horse-chestnut or the pheasant's-breast.

Her elder sisters had fine long hair of a pale flaxen, and to them Edith's rich tresses were odious. They had regular features, slightly aquiline, a delicate bloom, and light blue eyes.

Edith had a broad full forehead, fine deep-set dark eyes, full of fire and feeling, and looking at that time much too large for the little pale, pointed face to which they belonged.

With regard to her figure: it was very small for her age, and threatened to be deformed by a curvature of the spine, and the shortening of one leg. And even the doctors could not decide positively what the result of the accident she had met with would be. A great accession of health and strength might enable her to recover entirely.

As it was, she was doomed to spend the livelong day on a reclining-board. And this necessity, which shut her out from all the pleasures and occupations of other children, would have been intolerable to her, but for the sympathy, companionship, and devoted kindness of Arthur Bertram, Mr. Croft's grandson.

The Croft children, headstrong, selfish, and quarrelsome, took little notice of poor Edith, who could not in any way contribute to their amusement.

But Arthur Bertram would sit by her reclining-board the livelong day, reading to her; for when Edith went to live at the Crofts' he was four years older than herself, very precocious in intellect, but rather a proud, sensitive boy, who preferred the company of the grateful and bright little invalid to that of the rude, jealous, bullying young Crofts.

Mrs. Croft was as good as her word; little Edith had every care and attention. She was made a great deal of, for she was the Earl of Rockalpine's grand-daughter, and had no little influence with the miserly old recluse, who, to please her, as she gained strength and was able to sit up and drive out, would invite her and her chosen friend Arthur to spend weeks together at the Castle; and Edith would sometimes get one or other of the Croft children included in the invitation, and induce her grandpapa to let Roger and some of his Eton schoolfellows, whom he invited during the holidays (always selecting the sons of the rich and affluent) to fish or shoot in the Rockalpine preserves.

Edith was fast growing straight, strong,

rosy, and very pretty; and a more charming little couple than Edith Lorraine and Arthur Bertram could not be found. And while they grow together in grace, goodness, and beauty, we must inquire what Lady Hauteville and her handsome daughters are doing in town; and how the presentation of the Misses Lorraine went off at her Majesty's Drawing-room.

CHAPTER VII.

"So full of dismal terror was the time."
SHAKESPEARE.

"With scores of ladies, whose bright eyes
Rain influence, and adjudge the prize."
MILTON.

WE have said that at the first Drawing-room of the season held by our beloved Queen (then a proud wife and a happy daughter), Lady Hauteville intended to present her two eldest girls, Miss Lorraine and Georgina Lorraine.

Miss Lorraine was eighteen; and seventeen (which was her sister's age) is that which Fashion has fixed for that ceremony, which is, as it were, the inauguration of young English ladies of the "upper ten thousand" into fashionable life.

It is an anxious and important event to all mothers and daughters. Of course it is much more so among the aspiring classes (whose predecessors in the female line have not had the honour of bending the knee to, and kissing the hand of, the queens of other days) than it can be to those "born to tread the crimson carpet, and to breathe the perfumed air," and to whom presentation at Court comes as a natural event, and almost as a birthright. But still, even to the loftiest, it is an event of importance. The young beauty, whom the wise Belgravian mamma has so carefully kept from the eyes of those whose fiat decides her rank as a belle, lest the great charm of novelty should be worn off, is now exhibited for the first time to the world of Fashion, and that in the searching glare of the mid-day sun; and bare-headed, and her neck, her arms, and shoulders uncovered—in short, in an evening dress, which a wag once severely called almost a dress of Eve—is, as it were, put up in the matrimonial market.

For what else in reality is this introduction into society? And what are all the rich old beaux (whether widowers or bachelors), "who from sordid parents buy the loathing virgin," but bidders—the highest bidders, perhaps—in that market, and those to whom the youngest and loveliest are sure to be "knocked down?"

Lady Hauteville was, as we have said, a *parvenue;* and though a very clever one, and a very adroit imitator of the calm self-possession and high-bred indifference of the fair patricians around her, she was not, as they were, exactly what she seemed. In reality, she was very much excited at the idea of presenting her daughters.

She was in an inward fever about their dress, their appearance, and the effect they would produce. Her eldest was rather backward, both in the development of her person and her mind; while the second was precocious, at least as far as the former is concerned. And therefore it was that Lady Hauteville had decided to give Miss Lorraine the advantage of another year, hoping she would fill out into greater roundness, and have more manner, and more to say for herself, and be even then not more of a woman than her sister at seventeen.

She had acted wisely. Miss Lorraine, who at seventeen had been lank and scraggy, with very thin arms and red elbows, a very flat bust, and a tendency to purple arms and a red nose, shy, nervous, silent, and awkward, at eighteen was a well-rounded, graceful creature, with white hands and a white nose, easy manners, and plenty to say.

It was a very gay Drawing-room. Victoria, every inch a Queen, although those inches be not many, but looking taller than she is, stood with her noble Consort close at hand, the soft spring sun sparkling in her jewels, and a bright light and a soft beam in her large blue eyes, whenever any fair young *débutante* bent tremblingly before her.

Fair Queen! the Angel of Death had not then left the shadow of his dark wings on her heart or hearth; she had never known a real woe. Alas! alas! how has she wept since that bright day! May He who sent the dread, fierce sorrow enable her to bear it, and in His mercy temper the wind to the shorn lamb.

But to our tale. Lady Hauteville, although all rich brocade and gorgeous colours, and flashing gems herself, was well aware that an elegant simplicity best becomes the spring-time of beauty. Autumn has her gorgeous velvet dahlias; spring has her pale primroses, her snowdrops, her soft lilies.

Among those presented at that Drawing-room, the Misses Lorraine were pre-eminent for that fair, delicate, proud, patrician beauty, which is almost peculiar to our young female aristocracy. They were—as *débutantes* always should be—in pure white; their glacé silk trains were ornamented with bouquets of lilies of the valley, white roses, and stephanotis; their many-skirted tulle dresses were looped up with the same. They wore no ornaments but pearls; long and ample white tulle veils hung like a soft vapour about them; a pearl tiara was on each fair brow; a plume of white feathers waved gracefully from each blonde head, and drooped on to the white shoulder. The excitement of the occasion flushed their cheeks with a becoming and delicate rose tint; and they had been so well tutored and trained by Monsieur Le Zephyr, their dancing-master, that they made no mistake of any kind, but backed adroitly and gracefully out of the Queen's presence, having taken with precision and success their first step in high life, and having been, in fact, *presented!*

Lord and Lady Hauteville, who, as he was a minister, had the privilege of the *entrée,* joined their fair daughters in the lobby.

Lord Hauteville was always silent, pale, reserved, and pre-occupied. He went through his part at the Drawing-room like an automaton. His thoughts were far away; perhaps they were hovering round a certain little, grassy amphitheatre, fenced in by firs and other evergreens, in a dark wood, three hundred miles away. Perhaps a certain fir-tree, with some deadly, and to him, appalling symbols carved on its bark, rose on his mental vision. Perhaps certain withered and discoloured patches on the soft, green sod that carpeted the spot, forced themselves on his memory, and brought with them maddening recollections of blood—a brother's blood! Perhaps that scene recalled a *levée* at which, twenty years before, his elder brother, then Lord Hauteville, and himself, had been presented.

Quite against his will, and in spite of himself, all the past might have come back upon his mind; and the late noble form of his brother—his fine face, full of life, and hope, and love—have come before him, and shut out his gorgeous, triumphant wife, those fair and proud young beauties (his daughters), and all the young, meaningless, and blooming, and the old, haggard, and worn-out faces of those who crowded round to congratulate, to admire, or to criticise.

Among those who pressed round to admire were the old Earl of Richlands, a childless and almost childish widower; the young Marquis of Malplaquet, a red-haired, long-backed noodle, with a hollow roof and a hollow heart; Sir Joseph Brownlow, a millionaire, who had made his fortune by speculation, and who was of low birth, red face, vulgar person and habits, sordid mind, and middle age; but yet was an object of constant aim and vivid interest to Belgravian mammas, and—alas! that we should be obliged to own it—to their daughters, too!

There was, also, a very handsome, dark, moustachioed count, tall, slender, looking like a hero of a novel, who, from a little distance, was shooting dark glances at Miss Lorraine. He was an Italian, who called himself Romeo de Roccabella. He had been presented at a *levée*, by an English nobleman, with whom he had been intimate in Italy, and to whom he had rendered some service, and therefore he found no difficulty in getting to the Drawing-room.

This Italian had constantly met the Misses Lorraine taking their early morning walk in the park, before breakfast, with their governess. He had been struck by their beauty, and had followed them home.

He had made inquiries, and had ascertained who and what they were; and they, on their side—with the curiosity of their age, the love of any sort of excitement that belongs to a life of enforced seclusion, and the romance that lurks even in the coldest female breast—had begun to anticipate meeting him in their morning walk—to speculate about him—to count up the times they had seen him—to comment on his looks and dress, and to interchange signs and whispers about him, when the weary, pale governess had dropped asleep, or had left the school-room for a few minutes of blessed quiet, freedom, and seclusion from them.

The inquiries of Count Romeo de Roccabella ended in his hearing an exaggerated account of the wealth of the Hauteville family, and, what interested him still more, that the two elder Misses Lorraine had each a fortune of twenty thousand pounds, left her absolutely by her millionaire grandfather, Sir James Armstrong, and which became her own on her attaining the age of twenty, or on her marrying, with the consent of her parents, before.

After this, the Count never once missed the morning walk in Kensington Gardens or Hyde Park, in which he was sure to meet the little, pale, dark, neat governess, and the two tall, blonde, fair young girls.

Nor was this all. He haunted the neighbourhood of their house. He prowled about the iron railings of the square, in which they sauntered with poor little Miss Lindley, their governess, every evening. He even contrived to borrow, against all rules, a key of the square gardens, from a friend whose mother lived in the square.

Georgina Lorraine thought he was her admirer. Augusta fancied it was she who had made this grand conquest; and even poor, little, dark, pale Miss Lindley, with her square face and spectacles, but with a neat little figure, and a pretty foot and ancle, and full of novels, in which governesses were the heroines, such as "The Life of a Lover," "The Daily Governess," "Jane Eyre," "Ann Sherwood," &c., &c., thought that she herself might, after all, be the attraction, and indulged in day and night dreams of a handsome husband, a home in some Italian palace, and freedom from the wearying, enervating drudgery of teaching.

The Count had contrived, by the offer of an umbrella (one day that it rained), and by picking up a book (perhaps purposely dropped), to scrape a sort of slight acquaintance with the young ladies and their governess. He had found out which was the elder of the two—with a view, we fear, of knowing which had the longest time to wait for her twenty thousand pounds.

And the result was, that all his dark glances were in future aimed at Miss Lorraine—and she, of course, fell desperately in love with him.

Lady Hauteville was overjoyed to see that the Earl of Richlands and the young Marquis of Malplaquet were, after they had been introduced by herself, paying assiduous court to her youngest daughter; while the millionaire, Sir Joseph, strained his round bloodshot eyes, and short, apoplectic neck, and rose on tip-toe (for he was very short), to address some vulgar personal compliments to Miss Lorraine. But she had no eyes nor ears except for the sighing, glancing Count, and answered Sir Joseph Brownlow with brief monosyllables and great incoherence. He, a vain, purse-proud old fool, attributed all this to timidity, and to the consciousness of being the object of the admiration of one of the greatest catch-matches of the season.

Lady Hauteville was in an inward ecstasy. She had already quite settled it in her own mind that her eldest daughter should become Lady Brownlow, with an almost fabulous fortune; and that her Augusta should be allowed to choose between the old Earl of Richlands and the young Marquis of Malplaquet.

The arrangements at St. James's are, as it is well known, anything but judicious. There is a terrible crush, and great destruction of finery, before getting into the royal presence; and the same passions agitate an aristocratic mob that excite a democratic one. Self reigns supreme, and elbowing is the order of the day.

That ordeal over, there is another and a

very protracted one, and which a little better management might greatly mitigate—that of getting your carriage. Bare-headed, bare-necked belles, of all ages, stand, closely jostled together, by the hour, just outside St. James's Palace, awaiting the announcement by the Queen's footmen, that their servants are in attendance, and ready to announce their carriages. Beaux become very anxious, fussy, and busy, and are perfectly useless.

The broad daylight out of doors is very trying to the temper and the complexion of all but the youngest and most gentle.

Lord Richlands looked much more made up, old, and grim, in the broad glare of day, than he had done in the softened light inside the palace.

Both he and the young Marquis were very officious about Lady Hauteville's carriage; and Sir Joseph Brownlow was in a perfect fume.

But yet it was a very long time before the burly coachman, in his wig, and the tall footmen, with their powdered heads, gorgeous liveries, gold-headed sticks, and huge, hothouse bouquets, appeared in view.

And all this time the fair young beauties gained in reputation for loveliness, for no daylight can reveal grey hairs, or wrinkles, or hollows, or rouge, or *Poudre Impératrice*, or false ringlets, or artificial charms of any kind, where they do not exist; and the Count de Roccabella, as he hovered near Miss Lorraine,. and saw the love-light in her large blue eyes, and read messages from the heart, written in blushes on her checks, began to find Interest and Inclination unite in his determination to marry her.

Sir Joseph Brownlow said to himself, "I've made an impression on that young beauty. No girl ever looked and blushed like that, unless something was busy at her heart, for the first time; and I won't stand shilly-shallying, either, till she's got a bevy of young coxcombs about her. I'll strike while the iron's hot; before a week passes over my head I'll propose—and in a month I'll show them a Lady Brownlow worth looking at!"

"Well, the girls *have* made a triumphant *début*, Hauteville," said my lady, the Belgravian mamma, as soon as they were safely shut into their splendid new carriage, and were slowly progressing back to Belgrave Square.

CHAPTER VIII.

"Why looks your grace so heavily to-day?"
SHAKESPEARE.

LORD HAUTEVILLE was by his lady's side in the front seat of the "Clarence;" the two Misses Lorraine were in the "beauty seat," *alias* the back seat. Miss Lorraine was in a sweet reverie; Augusta was enjoying the admiration of the "outsiders." Both were too much self-engrossed to notice that, although their father mechanically answered, or rather echoed, Lady Hauteville's remark in the words, "Very triumphant, indeed, my dear," there was a hoarse quaver in his voice, and that his face, alwys pale and stern, was positively livid; that his eyes glared wildly, as if he had seen a ghost, and that his white lips were compressed, as in great pain, while the lace ruffles of his Court dress quivered with the ague-like shiver that ran through his frame.

And what had the great man seen, to cause this abject terror?

Simply a bronzed, weather-beaten, rough-headed, sturdy fellow, with his wide-awake pulled down over his bushy brows, and his coloured choker drawn up to his mouth, but with enough of his dreaded, well-known face uncovered, for Lord Hauteville to recognise "Rough Rob;" while in the tall, elastic form at his side, and the face, and air, whose native beauty, character, and dignity, would have well become a train, a tiara, and a plume of feathers, and, so set off, would have eclipsed many of the proudest beauties he had just left behind, the pale, trembling Hauteville recognised Rough Rob's handsome Irish wife, Mary!

Lord Hauteville had hoped and believed that Rough Rob was, by this time, far away—that he was on the broad Atlantic, at least, if he had not already landed at New York, with the friends who were to join him in the speculation for which his lordship had furnished Rough Rob with the funds.

What could have detained him in London? And what could induce him to show himself in the broad light of day, and in so dense a crowd, risking detection, apprehension, trial, and the scaffold? At the thought, Lord Hauteville shook like an aspen leaf.

Rough Rob, innocent, and therefore fearless, took no precautions but those which his Mary enforced. He had still a great hankering after giving himself up, and standing his trial like a man. He was strong in a conviction that God would not allow an innocent man to be found guilty and to be hanged, nor the real murderer to escape the punishment of his crime.

"What if I be tooked and tried for my life, Mary!" he would say; "there's One above that cares even for a poor hunted cretur like I, and I ought to have trusted in Him, and have stood my trial like a man, and not have skulked off like a guilty wretch."

"Och hone!" his Mary would reply; "och hone, och hone! why will ye not be advised, Rob, whin the best frind ye has in the wide world say's ye'd be hanged like a dog! Surely my Lord must judge better than the likes of you. Ye'll break my heart wid yer daring ways, ye will. It 'ud kill me dead to have ye dragged to the gallows, and I'd never know a minute's pace after I was onst a a widow—no, not if I lived till a hundred. I'd never recover the shame; and my people, how they'd cast it up to me, that I ran away and got married to a gallows-bird. Och hone, och hone!"

With these and similar arguments, Mary induced Rough Rob to keep indoors a good deal (a great trial to the wild man of the woods), and when he could not bear to stay in, to conceal his person as much as he could.

An inevitable delay in the arrangements of Mike O'Rourke, had kept Rough Rob and his wife in St. Giles's. But they were to set sail for America on the very night of the day on which the Queen held her first Drawing-room for that year at St. James's.

Now, Mary had a cousin, who had bettered herself—had married a rising man, who had met with great luck in life; and a letter from Ireland brought the news that Mary's cousin, once her equal, her playfellow, her confidante, Nora O'Halloran, who had married Lawyer O'Hara, now Sir Miles O'Hara, was to be presented at Court, "and wear a long thrain and fine feaders, and jowels, and all to knale down before the Queen, and kiss her Majesty's hand."

Mary felt no envy of her cousin Nora's prosperity, although the contrast in the lot of the two beauties, who had been girls together (and Mary much the handsomer of the two) would force itself on her mind; but she felt a great desire, an intense curiosity, to see Lady O'Hara in her Court dress; and Rob, finding out this, her secret wish, overmastered her fears, and resolved she should see all that could be seen, by early taking up their place in St. James's Street. And Mary did see her cousin; Mary, the head of her grey cloak drawn over her bonnet, and her features concealed as much as possible; Mary, in her Irish peasant costume, much the worse for wear, clinging, with love's strength, to Rough Rob, the suspected murderer, the escaped prisoner, for whose apprehension a thousand pounds was offered. Rough Rob, with a price upon his head, and Nora, sparkling with jewels, her white plumes heaving in the breeze, looking all pride and triumph, with a little, mean-looking, sly, ugly old man by her side, on whom she looked down, for she was much taller than he was, and who was jealous of every man that glanced at her, and seemed in a very ill-humour. And in spite of her jewels, her feathers, her rich white satin train, and her pride, there was a dreary discontent in Nora's face, and she answered her jealous lord sharply, and there was cold scorn in the glance with which she met his suspicious scrutiny; and seeing this, Mary clung more closely to Rough Rob, and looking up into his eyes, with tears of tenderness in her own, she said,

"Och, Rob! Rob! there goes Nora in all her splendour, her jowels, and her feaders, her thrain and her cooch; and for all that, I'd not change places wid her! She can't love the little, jeilous Hop-o'-my-thumb by her side. He distrusts her, and she despises him. I'd rather stand here on fute, wid my own poor, innocent, wronged, and hunted Rob, and feel I'm all the world to him, and him to I, than be a grand lady, going to Court in my cooch, by the side of the likes of Lawyer O'Hara."

It was while Mary spoke thus—her fine grey eyes full of tears, raised to Rough Rob's face, and his, moist, too, with dews from the heart, bent down upon her—that the Hauteville equipage moved slowly by them, and thus they did not see his lordship—their "best friend and noble pathron," as they called him in the ignorance and simplicity of their hearts.

It was a great relief to Lord Hauteville that they did not see him. But the sight of them disturbed his peace by day, and his sleep by night. For many a long day after, when in his lonely chamber, he woke from a troubled sleep, in which his hot breast seemed to be trampled on by the sharp hoofs of a whole stud of nightmares, to lie in a cold perspiration, shaking the stately bed, with the velvet hangings, surmounted by a coronet. A scaffold would weave itself into the coats-of-arms on the velvet and on the chair backs; and the Past would rise on his memory with all the freshness of yesterday. He would see the little grassy amphitheatre in the Black Wood, and his brother, with the life-blood purpling the grass, and that small, spectral, scarlet rill, that would trickle down the gentle slope, and, as it were, give him chase. And then Fancy dissolved that view, and he saw a dark mob of countless heads, and heard low groans of execration, and shouts and yells, and he was mounting, with ice-cold feet, the steps of the scaffold; and the white cap was drawn over his face, and the cord was adjusted round his neck, and all was over in this world. But the next? Oh! Fancy dared not picture the eternity of the fratricide.

And while her lord, in his lonely chamber, was suffering the tortures of the damned, Lady Hauteville, in her soft lace cap, with its pink rosettes, and her richly-embroidered night-gear, was smiling in her sleep, as she dreamt of the gay weddings of the future Lady Brownlow, and that of the Countess of Richlands, or the Marchioness of Malplaquet, she did not care which, for if the Marquis was a grade higher in rank, the Lord of Richlands had finer estates, the handsomer town mansion in Grosvener Square, and the more splendid family diamonds. Besides, he had been married, and knew what a lady of fashion required, and had been very liberal, in every way, to the late countess; while the Marquis of Malplaquet, though so young, and a *roué*, was a sordid one. He was known to be mean; indeed, his stinginess about settlements had caused the breaking off of a match between him and a belle of the preceding season.

And after all Lady Hauteville did not care which of these two noble and ignoble suitors led her fair Georgina to the altar, but lay on her bed of down, smiling in her sleep, under the influence of the spirit of fashion, which

> "Oft in dreams invention may bestow,
> To add a flounce or change a furbelow."

And so this time the partner of her life—he whom she had taken for better, for worse, and had sworn to keep in sickness and in health, in weal or woe, till death did them part—lay, in a room separated from hers only by a dressing-closet, lying on that rack which a guilty conscience spreads upon every bed of "stubble or of stubble-down;" cold drops of sweet upon his brow, "the worm that dieth not" feeding on his heart, and the fire that is not quenched scorching his brain.

Oh! who that could count the cost would ever stain his hands with blood, and sell his soul to the great enemy of mankind, who is ever at hand, first to tempt to crime, and then to exult in the anguish it entails, and the hideous penalties it enforces?

CHAPTER IX.

> "Oh, there's nothing half so sweet in life
> As Love's young dream."
>
> MOORE.

ONCE fairly launched in the world of fashion, the Misses Lorraine, like all the other belles of Belgravia and fair of Mayfair, resolved to drain the cup of pleasure to the dregs.

They were reigning belles. They dressed, danced, rode, flirted, to perfection; they waltzed or polked all night, and yet were in their cold baths at eight, and in the parks betimes in the morning, riding in search of the roses of health.

They ate like troopers at that substantial early dinner which the gay world calls a luncheon. They sipped their cheering, refreshing five o'clock tea, with its relays of delicate toast and thin bread-and-butter, in Lady Hauteville's boudoir; and talked over their own conquests and charms, and the failures and faults of their rivals, and decided what dresses they should wear, and in what style their hair should be done; and then they were able at an eight o'clock dinner to pretend to live upon air, and, not to offend the refined taste of some high-bred exquisite, by any display of a natural appetite, to confine themselves to nibbling a bit of chicken, or trifling with a *soufflé*, a jelly, an ice, or some choice fruit.

The Count di Roccabella, although never invited by Lady Hauteville to any *soirée*, or "at home" at her own house, contrived to meet Miss Lorraine at balls and parties; and, all insolent, haughty, and self-possessed as she had become (taking her tone from the society in which she moved), she could "bate her proud looks" to him, even though the Earl of Richlands had proposed and been accepted. Lady Hauteville had laughed her daughter out of all scruples, all objections to the old *ci-devant* Adonis, old enough to be her father. The liberal settlements, the wedding presents, the *trousseau*, the jewels, the equipages, were the talk of the *beau monde*, and the envy of the belles.

The Count looked despair and suicide.

Lord Richlands wanted an early day fixed, but Miss Lorraine was resolved not to put on the galling golden fetters till she had enjoyed one season in town; and the wedding was to take place at the end of June. Meanwhile she gave herself up to dissipation, perhaps to silence the "still small voice" that will be heard in solitude.

Sir Joseph Brownlow and the young Marquis of Malplaquet had not come forward as

Lady Hauteville had expected they would. A new beauty—a sparkling, lively little brunette—had made her *début* since the "Lorraine girls," and the old Earl and the young Marquis forsook the blonde, inanimate Augusta.

Lady Hauteville would have been in despair but for Georgina's splendid prospects. And now the last grand *fête* at which the bride-elect was to appear before that brief seclusion which approaching wedlock entails was about to "come off" at Lady Louisa Seymour's villa at Twickenham. It consisted of a *matinée*, which began at three p.m., a dinner-party, and a ball.

The weather was exquisite, and the heat intense. The gardens were illuminated by coloured lamps, and still more by the silver moon. Lady Hauteville, who was confined to her room by a cold, accepted for her daughters the chaperonage of the Duchess of Snowdon. Lord Richlands, to his great grief, could not escort his bride-elect; business connected with his marriage had summoned him to Richlands Park.

Georgina's heart beat high, for she knew—but how we cannot reveal—that Count Romeo di Roccabella was to be at this *fête*.

Oh! wretched, weak, guilty girl, victim of a false and heartless system! She, the bride-elect, is in a secret tumult of joy, because the Count will be present, and her intended will be far away.

The *matinée* passed off wearily to the bride-elect, nor less so to Augusta Lorraine, who was doomed, in spite of a new and most elegant toilette, to see the old Baronet and the young Marquis devote themselves to Brillanté de Beauvoir, the sparkling brunette, with so much to say, and so much *à la mode*, who had brought dark beauty into fashion, and without a tithe of the personal charms of the blonde Lorraines, had, with her saucy little Roxalana nose, put the delicate aquilines of Augusta and Georgina quite out of joint, as the Earl would have said, only that he, at least, poor fellow! was faithful to fair beauty, for he was really in love with a blonde.

Poor Georgina! she was beginning to feel very sick at heart. The dinner passed heavily off; the ball began, and still he came not. The Duchess of Snowdon, the Lorraines' chaperon, sat down to whist; the company in the intervals of the dance, spread over the grounds. Georgina's impatience and disappointment became unbearable. She watched her opportunity, and just as the dance recommenced, she slipped out at a glass door, and hurried away, to hide the tears she could not repress, in a dark shrubbery that skirted the river.

She had not been there long when she heard the splashing of oars, and a voice, that made her heart bound and her cheeks glow, sang *A te, o cara*, in a voice which—

> "—— Music to the ear,
> Became a memory to the soul."

"He is come! he is come!" she whispered to herself, wildly clasping her hands. "I will see him! I must speak to him! I must tell him my heart is his, although I am compelled to give my hand to another!"

She rushed out of the shrubbery, and found the Count, who had just landed from a boat, standing near a marble urn.

"You are come," she said; "come at length!" and there were tears in her voice.

He drew her arm in his, and led her back into the shrubbery. There, in language full of passionate eloquence, he told her that he adored her; he painted to her a life of misery with her intended—of purest happiness with him. He told her he was there, not to see her for a moment, and then to leave her for ever, but to bear her away with him to his own sweet, sunny Italy, there to devote his whole life to love and her!

"My mamma!" faltered the distracted girl.

"Mamma!" he cried. "Why, she would sell your youth, your beauty, and your warm, young heart, for gold. I have arranged all. I have a licence ready. To-morrow, before a registrar, I will make you my wife—my countess—the Countess di Roccabella! and the ceremony in our respective churches can be performed abroad."

"But I am not of age! A marriage will not be valid, will it, Romeo?"

"Oh! yes. No one will dispute it; when it is once done, they will make the best of it; and we shall be far, far away. I have a boat and two men close by; they will bear us to a spot where a carriage-and-four awaits us. Nay, nay, I will hear no objections, no scruples, *carissima!* If you refuse, you do not love me, and I will die."

"I love you too well!" sobbed Georgina.

"Then prove it, angel! Queen of my soul! idol of my heart! Come! fly with your Romeo—like a second Juliet, fly with me!"

So saying, and using a gentle force, the Count led the pale, bewildered, weeping, but enraptured girl to the boat, with one hand clasping her white arm, and another half encircling her waist; he got her to the boat just as some ladies among the guests, who had failed to secure partners, came out to look at the moon and stroll about the grounds.

They did not recognise the lovers, for Georgina Lorraine had thrown a scarf over her head, and of her tall graceful figure they only saw the back; but there was an earnestness in the dark-mantled, pale-faced, moustachioed cavalier, which arrested their attention and interested their feelings; and so from a little distance, they watched what they little suspected was the elopement of the envied bride-elect of the millionaire, the Earl of Richlands, with a penniless Italian adventurer, who, though he admired her beauty, and felt flattered by her love, was chiefly urged on by the thought of the twenty thousand pounds which in less than two years would be hers, and therefore his.

It was not till the ball broke up at 4 A.M., and Miss Lorraine could nowhere be found, that these ladies began to understand what they had seen. And then, not wishing, as they said, to be brought forward and get into trouble, they decided on saying nothing that could throw any light on the mysterious disappearance of the bride-elect, Miss Lorraine.

CHAPTER X.

> "Alas! that this should ever be—
> Gold thus o'er Faith and Love prevailing;
> Great curse! where shall we flee from thee,
> Since even Woman's faith is failing?"
>
> L. E. L.

BITTER indeed was the disappointment of the haughty *parvenue*, Lady Hauteville, when it became known to herself, and to that world for which alone she lived, that her favourite daughter (on the eve of becoming an English Countess) had eloped with an Italian adventurer.

Her grief was not the natural grief of a tender mother, ruthlessly robbed of a beloved and loving child, trembling for her dear one's fate, dreading the retribution always in store for a disobedient and ungrateful daughter, and the punishment generally inflicted by the very hand which has led her astray! No; her grief was made up of rage, wounded vanity, mortified pride, disappointed ambition. She had so revelled in her anticipated triumph over Belgravian mammas of higher birth and far more thorough-bred feelings and manners than herself, whose daughters "hung on hand" (as the match-makers say), and who, having passed through the cold spring, the sunless summer, and the gloomy autumn of their charms, saw the "winter of their discontent" coming on with their eight-and-twentieth year. For the career of an unmarried belle in the world of fashion cannot be allowed to exceed ten seasons, after which time she dwindles into a "has been," and is fairly, or rather unfairly shelved. We say unfairly; for many women are lovelier and more loveable at seven-and-twenty than at seventeen. But there must be *mind*, to replace the first lustre of youth in the eyes; feeling, to animate the cheeks with blushes dearer than the rosy tints of dawn; a riper loveliness must enrich the form, to atone for the loss of the sylphide beauty of girlhood; and the expression, manners, and conversation, must have gained in grace, dignity, and sympathy what they have lost in sprightliness, *naïveté*, and archness.

Lady Hauteville's distress was all the deeper and the more unbearable, on account of the hollow, sham condolences and ill-veiled exultation of those who had angled in vain for the rich old Earl of Richlands, for their own daughters.

Then, too, Augusta was no longer the fashion, and Ida was not yet out. Of Edith, the worldly, ambitious mother only thought as "the carroty cripple," who had better live on with the Croft family, a cripple in childhood, youth, womanhood, and old age, if it were not wisely decreed that she should be removed from a world in which (as her cold mother said) her existence was a burthen to herself and her friends. For what a blighted being must a carroty cripple be! For *her* there could be no "season," no presentation at Court, no introduction into the world of fashion.

A letter from Mrs. Croft was lying on the breakfast-tray, which had just been brought to Lady Hauteville's bedside. The miserable Belgravian mamma had not been able to summon energy to rise.

"Send Miss Augusta to me, Leno," she said to her maid; and she began to dip her strips of toast in her chocolate.

Miss Augusta knocked at the door.

"Come in," said Lady Hauteville, languidly. "Leave us, Leno. I will ring when I want you."

Leno retired, but only into a closet, where,

concealed behind some ample dresses, she could hear all that passed.

"Good Heavens! how pale and sallow you look, Augusta!" exclaimed the mamma; "and how frightfully your hair is done!"

"Céleste has dressed my hair exactly as you directed her, mamma. I own I thought it very unbecoming; but she said she had your orders, and of course they were her law and mine."

"Of course; but now I order you and Céleste to return to your former style. That lovely brunette, Brillanté de Beauvoir, looked so exquisite with her glossy black hair *à l'Eugenie*, and the Marquis of Malvoisin—and, in fact, all the *best* men—were so smitten with her, I thought if you adopted that style it might bring you a few of her rejected suitors. But I see it won't do. Your forehead is too high, your nose too sharp, and your features too marked for it;

besides, your eyes are red, and you look positively haggard!"

"It is now three days and nights since Georgina went away," said Augusta, her eyes filling with tears, "and nothing has been heard of her. And there are reports, I find from Céleste, that this Italian is an adventurer, and no Count at all; and that he has eloped with Georgina for the sake of the fortune grandpapa left her. And——"

"Pray don't bring me all the tittle-tattle of the servants'-hall, and, perhaps, the kitchens. If true, your ungrateful, treacherous, and worthless sister is rightly punished. I have driven her from my thoughts—my heart" (and the lady pressed her white hand to the bosom of her embroidered night-dress, on the vacant place where a heart should have been), "and I command you to do the same."

"But we were always together. From my

birth I never was a day or night away from Georgina, until that dreadful *fête*. If I knew that she was happy, I could bear it better."

Here the poor girl's sobs got the better of her fear of her mother, and she walked to the window, and hid her face in her handkerchief. She was startled presently by her mother's voice, in its angriest tones.

"Augusta," she said, "let us understand one another. Your sister has acted basely, cruelly, vilely, both by me and by her noble intended; and if you, instead of doing all you can to console me, and to atone for her degrading choice, by making a brilliant match yourself, are going to fret yourself into a frightful red-eyed spectre, about a sister who never loved you, but who was very jealous of and spiteful to you—say so; and I shall not remain in London to witness such insane folly. I shall go at once down to Armstrong Hall or Rockalpine; and there you can weep away to your heart's content. Ida, as you well know, cannot be introduced till next spring, and she is getting on so well at Hyde Park House, that I shall not remove her. I have no daughter, then, to comfort me, but you; and unless you promise me to forget all about your unprincipled sister, and to try all you can to make a brilliant match, to atone to me for this disappointment, I shall leave town to-morrow for Armstrong Hall."

Augusta, though she had some natural feelings left, was still a belle of Belgravia. "The season" was everything to her. The solitude of Armstrong Hall, with her bitter, taunting, and exasperated mamma as her companion, was intolerable. She had not even the governess to turn to, for she had been discharged when Augusta had completed her seventeenth year.

"I will do my best to obey you, mamma," she said, drying her eyes; "I know Georgina has acted very shamefully; I will try to atone to you for her disobedience."

"Sensibly spoken," said the mamma. "What's done can't be undone. I hope, for the family credit's sake, things may not turn out so bad as they seem. If the man is really an Italian count, even if he is (as of course he must be) a fortune-hunter, and, to some extent, an adventurer, all we can do is to make the best of it; but until we hear from the wretched fool herself, we can know nothing about it. Your papa was for pursuing and separating them, as she is a minor; but those things never answer—they make a great *esclandre;* parents have a disgraced and dishonoured daughter thrown back on their hands; no one else will marry her; and thus she is for life an eyesore, a dead weight, and a great expense. No; I have decided to let matters take their course. And now, what say you, my love, to the Earl of Richlands for yourself?"

Augusta shuddered and turned pale. Lady Hauteville did not appear to notice the effect of her suggestion.

"The dear old fellow once told me," said the mamma, "that it was quite a chance which of the *belles blondes* he proposed to; for he thought you like two lilies on one stalk—two pearls in one bed of cotton. Now, I think that a little sympathy at this crisis would bring him to your feet, and the triumph and delight of the Rosevilles, the Belmonts, the Roscommons, the Irelings, and the Fitzarthurs, would be turned to woe and envy. They are all spreading their nets already. Write him a little note, my love, and ask him to come and dine quietly with mamma and yourself, and then go alone with us in a private box to see Charles Kean in his great character of *Othello*. Richlands will take it kind; and I think if we don't do something of the sort, Lady Elfrida Belmont, or that sly Rhoda Roscommon, will get hold of him, and he'll be engaged to one of them before he knows what he is about. So write, my love, one of your pretty little coaxing notes; my darling knows exactly what to say."

Augusta bowed her head, and, with a heavy sigh, was about to leave the room to do her mother's bidding, and write to the old earl, when that lady, holding back the crimson velvet curtains of her bed with her delicate hand, said:

"Don't leave me just yet, my Gussy! You can write presently; but now I want you to read me this letter from Mrs. Croft. I suppose it is something about Edith—some new irons, or fresh doctor, or backboards, or systems to be tried. At any rate, I must know what it is; so read it to me."

Augusta took the letter, and read as follows:

"Croft Villa, near Alnwick, Northumberland.
"November 12th, 18—.

"MY DEAR LADY HAUTEVILLE,

"First allow me to congratulate you on the brilliant marriage which I see by the *Morning Post* and the *Court Journal* Miss Lorraine is about to contract. I have no doubt her lovely sister, Miss Augusta, will soon follow so good an example, and that the fair image of yourself, the beautiful Miss Ida, will, in due time, introduce a third coronet into your noble family. And now to business. I know you will rejoice to hear that your delicate darling and ours—sweet little Edith—is daily gaining strength and health. No remains of curvature of the spine is now apparent. The darling young lady can walk with ease and grace; but of course we do not allow her to indulge in any exertion which might produce relapse. Miss Edith is now, as you know, fourteen; and I have attended to her education as much as her delicate health permitted. But I am going to take my family abroad for three years. We shall embark from Sunderland in a yacht, which Mr. Croft has purchased at the sale of the late Duke of N——. We intend visiting Norway, Denmark, and Sweden, during the summer. We shall winter in Italy. I mean, during our stay abroad, to visit, with my family, all the cities of Europe, and make such a stay in the principal ones as will enable the young people to master the French, German, Italian, and Spanish languages.

"Dr. Bliss says that such a tour, as the one we propose, would be the very best thing possible for Miss Edith; and I now write to ask you and my Lord Hauteville to allow her to be of the party. With regard to the outlay,

Mr. Croft will communicate with my lord; but we shall travel so economically, that I think the liberal sum you now kindly remit quarterly will very nearly cover Miss Edith's expenses.

"Lord Rockalpine, who continues in his usual health, and takes great interest in the welfare of Miss Edith, highly approves of our scheme, and says, if he were a younger man, he would be of the party.

"Should your ladyship agree to our plan, we shall set off by water, from Sunderland, on this day week; and if not, I must beg you kindly to send a competent person to take charge of Miss Edith, as I cannot delay my departure.

"With best respects to the fair young bride-elect and her sweet sister,

"I remain, my dear madam,

"Your ladyship's most devoted servant,

"ANN CROFT."

"Of course I shall agree at once," said Lady Hauteville. "What could I do with the poor little carroty cripple? What competent person have I got to send for her? And where could she reside? No; I think it's a capital plan."

"But, mamma, if she has no remains of the curvature, and can walk with ease and grace, she cannot be a cripple now."

"Nonsense! She is, and was, and always, will be a cripple. Dr. Dulcibel said so, and he never makes a mistake. That's all boast and bravado of Mrs. Croft's, just to exalt herself, and the care she has taken of poor little Edith. Let me see; Ida will be seventeen next spring, and Edith is now fourteen. Not that Edith's age matters—I could never introduce a cripple—but Ida's does; and you, my darling, must contrive to get off before Ida comes out; for she's very pretty, and so much in your own style that you wouldn't have a chance. But now, for a short time, you've the field to yourself; so play your cards well, my love."

"What cards have I, mamma?"

"Youth, beauty, position, and, that queen of trumps, a sensible mother, my pet. And now go, write to the Earl, as I suggested; and then write for me to Mrs. Croft, and say that I highly approve of the Continental scheme, and shall be very glad to let Edith be of the party. We must dine at six. Tell the Earl to be in time for 'Othello'; and do you come down to tea with me at five, aud I will advise you what to wear. So cheer up, my love; you are my only hope and comfort now, and will be till next season, when Ida comes out; and all the presents I had meant for your ungrateful, treacherous sister shall be yours. I have in that drawer some such exquisite things, which I will show you at our five o'clock tea! Are you going to ride to-day?"

"I hate riding alone, mamma. I have no one to ride with."

"Never mind; go and take a country ride, and when you come in, have a bath, and go to bed for a few hours; you will then get up as fresh as a rose. Or, suppose you ask Miss de Belton to ride your sister's horse, and canter off to Clapham, and order some flowers from Acre. Not that it matters about a companion, with such a steady, experienced groom as James. But, do as you like, only do take your ride, your bath, and your siesta. And mind Céleste does your hair in the usual style. Richlands likes to see it waving round the face, so let it down again."

The obedient daughter left the Belgravian Mamma to finish her breakfast, and repaired to her escritoire, to write to the Earl and Mrs. Croft, and then, with a sigh, sent to offer Georgina's horse to Miss de Belton for a country ride. The offer was gladly accepted.

Augusta returned cheered and rosy from her long canter, and found on the hall-table a note in a tremulous hand from the old Earl, gallantly accepting the invitation to dinner and to escort the ladies to the play.

Augusta, full of Miss de Belton's aspirations after a coronet, and her wonder at Georgina's romantic folly, began to enter fully into her mother's plans. Augusta was imitative and impressionable; and the worldly maxims of Miss de Belton, a Belgravion belle of five years' standing, had quite turned the current of her thoughts. Georgina's love match had tinged them with romance, but now they were all worldly.

She took the bath and the siesta prescribed by her mamma, and again the softening influence of her silken blonde hair (its ripples touched with pale gold, and two love locks on her shoulders) was lent to her delicate, aristocratic, and now blooming face.

When Augusta entered her mother's boudoir to partake of her five o'clock tea, Lady Hauteville thought that her daughter's white tulle, many skirted dress over white glacé, and adorned with blue convolvoli, while a wreath of the same encircled her head, forming a diadem on her fair brow, and heightening the beauty of her light hair and fair complexion, were so perfect in taste and in effect, that she could suggest no improvement; only when Augusta produced the few tremulous, slanting lines of the old Earl, her mother went to her drawers, and, taking out a jewel-case of maroon morocco, displayed an exquisite set of sapphires and pearls; and calling Leno to put in the earrings, and to fasten the necklace, bracelets, and brooch, she said, embracing her delighted daughter (Leno having retired to her closet),

"I meant these for the future Countess of Richlands, and I fancy, in giving them to you, my love, I have about hit the mark."

Everything turned out as Lady Hauteville had planned and expected.

The old Earl's heart, unlike our Crystal Palace season tickets, *was* transferable. He was bent on marrying a young beauty. He was anxious to have an heir, to disappoint a nephew who had caricatured him. Augusta was quite as eligible in his eyes as Georgina.

The whole matter was kept very close, for Lady Hauteville had an acute sense of the fitness of things, and a great dread of ridicule, and this sudden transfer of the old Earl from one daughter to another would be, she well knew, while the matter was still pending, a standing joke at the clubs and in the *salons* of Belgravia and Mayfair. Once done, all would be anxious to pay their court to the young Countess of Richlands. Lady Hauteville, therefore, kept her own counsel.

The marriage was a very quiet one. It

took place at Armstrong Hall, and the *beau monde* knew nothing about it, until one morning in July, when most people had left town, and the flies were buzzing about the bald heads of the old heroes of the "Rag and Famish," the papers announced the marriage of the Right Honourable Felix, Earl of Richlands and Ross, to Augusta, second daughter of Lord and Lady Hauteville, aud granddaughter of the Right Honourable the Earl of Rockalpine. The *Court Journal* entered into greater details, and said the marriage ceremony was performed at Bagshot Church, that a few select friends and relatives partook of an elegant *déjeûner* at Armstrong Hall, the seat of Lord and Lady Hauteville, and that soon after the collation the happy pair set off for the Continent, *viâ* Folkestone, intending to spend the honeymoon in Switzerland, and at the German spas.

CHAPTER XI.

"But sweeter far than this—than these—than all—
Is first and passionate Love. It stands alone,
Like Adam's recollection of his fall.
The tree of knowledge has been stripped—all's known,
And Life yields nothing further to recall
Worthy of this ambrosial sin, so shown,
No doubt, in fable as the unforgiven
Fire Prometheus filch'd for us from Heaven."

BYRON.

THE time upon which Mrs. Croft had fixed for her continental tour was that of the midsummer vacation at Eton.

Her eldest son, it is true, had left school, and had matriculated at Oxford; but Clarissa's boy, Arthur, Mr. Croft's grandson, was to be of the travelling party; and he, too, was an oppidan at Eton.

To Mrs. Croft, and to all who interested themselves in Mr. Croft's affairs, it seemed very absurd in him to give to the poor boy whom he had adopted out of charity (the offspring of an undutiful daughter's clandestine marriage) the advantages which many gentlemen are obliged to deny even to their eldest sons —an education at Eton and Oxford. But on this subject Mr. Croft was immoveable, and, indeed, he had sternly forbidden Mrs. Croft to meddle in matters she did not understand; while to officious visitors who presumed to disapprove, he coldly remarked that "every man was the best judge of his own affairs, and that when he needed advice he would ask for it."

After this, no one presumed to express an opinion, or to offer any advice as to the education of young Bertram. They contented themselves with casting up their hands and eyes, and with whispering two very unpleasing and disparaging words, in reference to the poor departed Clarissa, and the beautiful and noble boy whom she had left to her father's care.

Nothing could exceed the delight of Edith Lorraine at the prospect of visiting all the beautiful countries and noble cities of which they had read together, in company with one whom she had always loved as a brother, until, with her fifteenth year, stole into the maiden's heart a feeling more subtle, more vague, more enchanting, than sisterly affection.

Arthur, nearly three years her senior, and consequently seventeen, had only just begun to feel his heart leap in his bosom at the sound of her voice, and his blood ebb and flow at the accidental touch of her little hand.

But the heart of woman ripens much sooner than that of man; and the maiden and her unacknowledged lover felt at the same

M 2

time the influence of him who "will be lord of all."

But as yet no suspicion of the power that bound them (as with a spell) had entered the heart or the mind of either. No thought of the Future, no plans, no prospects, no doubts, no fears, intruded on them in that freehold each young heart has, in the fairy land of Hope and Love. Indefeasible inheritance!—our little all of the Eden we lost through Sin, and which passes away from us as soon as Sin steals into the fairy bowers of Love, and the innocent heart of Youth.

Mrs. Croft had said truly, that there were no remains of the curvature of the spine, which had threatened with deformity the graceful shape of Edith Lorraine; no vestige of lameness remained, and her health and strength were entirely restored.

Mrs. Croft's cue was not, as Lady Hauteville imagined, to make Edith appear better and stronger than she was; but, on the contrary, to affect to consider her still as in a great degree an invalid, who might relapse into a cripple, and for whom change of air and scene was a great boon.

Mrs. Croft found the handsome stipend, which Lord Hauteville paid so regularly into her own hands, an inexpressible comfort and help, both to herself and to that aspiring youth, her son, whose great object was to be considered "fast"—an object not to be attained without a very great outlay.

The day before the departure of the Crofts, and of Edith Lorraine and Arthur, the old Earl of Rockalpine called at Croft Villa, to take leave of his grand-daughter, and to make her what, for him, was a magnificent present, namely, an old travelling-bag, which had been his mother's, curiously fitted up with toilet requisites of nearly a century back, and with silver and ivory handles."

When the old Earl arrived at Croft Villa, Arthur and Edith were roaming about the woods, taking a fond leave of scenes where they had been so happy. But Mrs. Croft received his lordship in her best drawing-room; and, while she went in search of Edith Lorraine, she proposed that her youngest child, a show-off, of the name of Gloriana, who was supposed to be a great musical genius, should entertain my lord by an exhibition of her talents on the piano. The old Earl had a keen sense of the ludicrous, and watched the little precocious caricature, at the piano, with a smile which the proud and enraptured mamma construed into admiration.

The old Earl of Rockalpine was come to take leave of his favourite grandchild Edith. He had listened with great patience to Glorian's grand .sonata, and had delighted both Mrs. Croft and the precocious young musician by his praises, and by a present of a sovereign to the young lady, to buy a keepsake in memory of himself. But when Edith came running in, out of breath with haste, and rosy as the Dawn, the Earl begged to be allowed to see his grand-daughter in private, and Mrs. Croft and Gloriana left the room.

Edith, although with the prospect of all the delights of novelty, change, new countries, and new people before her, and that, dearer still, of Arthur by her side to double and share every joy, could not choose but weep when the old Earl, with a softness and a feeling very unusual in one whose only affection for many years had been for his gold, took her in his arms, and stroking her bright, glossy, auburn head with his old withered hand, said,

"Farewell, my sunbeam!—my love!—my darling! I wish I were ten years younger, and then I would be of your party, my little one; for, indeed, the glory of poor grandpapa's sunset fades with your bright face and sunny smile, my precious little girl!"

"Oh! why cannot you come now, dear, dearest grandpapa?" said Edith, throwing her white arms round the old man's neck, and pressing her roseate cheek to his parchment yellow and wrinkled face, sere with age.

"No, my child. I am too infirm, too aged. Old trees, my pretty one, do not bear transplanting. And now, do not weep, my Edith, if I say that I fear I shall not see you again; but should it prove so—if the darkness that now and then overshadows my path, is, indeed, cast by the wings of the Angel of Death—if the rushing of those wings causes the chill, the shudder that occasionally thrills through me, icing the blood in my veins—then, my child (nay, do not sob) you will not see me on this earth again!"

"Oh, I *will* not go!" sobbed Edith; "I *will* stay with you—I *will* read to you—pray with you—sing to you—comfort you! How *can* I go away, and leave you to live and die alone?"

"Edith," said the old Earl, smiling, "I have read and re-read the little book you gave me; indeed, I know many of its hymns by heart. Now, listen.

"'Why should we faint and fear to live alone,
Since all alone—so Heaven had willed—we die?
Nor even the tenderest heart and next we own,
Knows half the reasons why we smile and sigh?

"'Each in his hidden sphere of joy or woe
Our hermit spirits dwell, and range apart;
Our eyes see all around in gloom or glow,
Hues of their own, fresh borrow'd from the heart!

"'And well it is for us our God should feel
Alone our secret throbbings: so our prayer
May readier spring to Heaven, nor spend its zeal
On cloud-born idols of this lower air.'

I know the hymn all through, my pretty one," added the Earl, "and I learned it to please you; but there is no time to say it now, for you have much to do, and I must return to the Castle; but before I go, sweet child, take an old man's thanks, an old man's blessing. Edith, till I knew you, and heard those truths which are hidden from the learned and the wise, proclaimed by you, then almost a babe, a suckling, and listened to hymns and prayers from your lips, I was living without God in the world! I had made an idol of gold, my love, and I worshipped it; but Heaven sent an angel, without wings, in your shape, my child, to lead me from darkness into light. Edith, I *was* an infidel—I *am* a believer, a penitent believer, and through you! So do not weep, my pretty one, your mission here is done. You have said, 'Awake, thou that sleepest, and arise from the dead, and Christ shall give thee life.' Do you remember where we were when you read that text to me, Edith?"

"We were sitting on some rocks by the sea," said Edith, very gently, looking up from the old man's bosom, on which her head was laid, and soft tears trickling down her cheeks. "There had been a terrible storm, grandpapa, and we had taken shelter in a cave, deep, deep in the rocks, and we had heard the thunder roar and reverberate through the caverns, and we had seen the forked lightning flash, and the rain beat down in torrents, and we drew closer together. It was so grand, so terrible, so awful a storm! And by degrees it abated. The rain ceased, the winds were hushed, the sun came out in all his glory; the rocks and the sands were soon dry, and a glorious rainbow spanned the sky. Its arch began on the horizon and ended on the keep of the castle tower; and we left our cave, and sat down by the sea on some masses of rock. They were warm in the sun, and countless beautiful shells and delicate seaweeds had been cast up by the waves, and I filled my basket with them, and I have them still. Oh, grandpapa, that storm and that heavy, awful darkness, and the fury of the elements, as we shrunk into the darkest corner of that cave, I never can forget; nor yet the heavenly calm that followed, the glorious sunshine, and that brilliant, beautiful rainbow!"

"Edith," said the old Earl, "I never told you before, but, on the eve of a long parting, I tell you now, my child, that that storm, that darkness, that calm, that sunshine, that rainbow, were symbols of what was passing in my soul at that time. Darker than that darkness had been my benighted spirit, when I entered that cave; fierce as the war of those elements was the contest going on within me; sudden as the gush of sunshine that followed, was the light of Grace shining into my soul; and bright and beautiful as that rainbow in the sky, was the bridge of penitence, pardon, and faith, by which my spirit was to mount to Heaven. When you prayed in the fervent piety of your pure young heart—when you prayed for deliverance from the perils of that storm, *I prayed too;* and when you returned thanks, *I joined you.* Edith, since I was a child at my mother's knee, until that hour in that cave with you, I had neither prayed nor thanked God for anything! And now prayer is my great solace; now I "search the Scriptures," as my little one told me I must do; now I live a new live; and now, instead of heaping up riches without knowing who shall gather them, I think night and day how I can bring a blessing on others, by the gold I have hoarded, and I mean to leave to Edith the power of dispensing my wealth for the good of the poor and needy."

"Oh, don't talk so—you will break my heart!" sobbed Edith, putting her little hand on his lips.

"Nay, you must hear me," said the Earl, kissing her finger-tips:—"you are my heiress, my sole executrix, my residuary legatee—everything that is not entailed, goes to you, my child! And if in the days to come, when you are a woman, my Edith, you wish to marry one worthy of you, in all but this world's dross, and friends would oppose and part you, and try to unite you to some vain, godless worldling who is rich and great, you can say, 'No; my grandpapa foresaw the trials that awaited me. He felt that I should wish to give my hand, where my heart had long been given; that I should prefer a good, noble Christian lover, whom I had known from childhood—(for had we not grown up together?)—who loved me for myself, to some titled coxcomb and spendthrift, who wedded me for connection or wealth. And he has empowered me to raise that dearest, truest one to my own level, and to select from the world, the Christian man of my heart to be the husband of my youth and the sharer of my good fortunes!' Ah! darling, never blush about it! Has old grandpapa discovered the dear delicious secret, scarcely known to her own heart, and never, never whispered to his?"

Edith, smiling through her tears, hid her face in the old man's breast. The Earl hugged her up, and continued:—

"They say there is a sort of second-sight given to those who are not long for this world; and I fancy I see my little Edith's future spread before her. And that noble youth, Arthur; I see he loves you, Edith, and I see that you love him; and whatever Worldliness may say about the disparity of birth and station between you, if you wed him you have your grandfather's blessing, for I see he is a true-hearted, noble-minded youth, and I see, too, in the distance, a halo around his head, independently of you, my Edith. That youth will be a great man; I cannot tell how or when it will come to pass, but I do clearly see a coronet on your Arthur's brow. Perhaps he is to achieve greatness; but be that as it may, I feel that he will be great, and that, in the end, those who have opposed and condemned will congratulate and approve. And now I go, my love; but not, as of yore, to a dreary solitude, with no companions but inanimate money-bags. No; my home now is the home of a Christian. Each hour has its pleasant Christian duty. In my Bible I have an inexhaustible source of comfort and interest, and this little book, this 'Christian Year,' your gift, is its fit companion—its handmaid. My solitary halls are no longer dark and dreary—the light of Grace is there; and I am no longer alone, for Faith is ever by my side."

Edith, still sobbing, slipped from the old Earl's breast, and fell on her knees before him.

"Don't weep, darling," he said, raising

her, "but listen:—your portrait, my Edith, stands on my table; your sweet face smiles on me, and your raised finger seems at one time to beckon, at another to warn. So do not weep, as if I were still the godless old miser going to count his hoards; I am now the aged Christian awaiting his summons. And now let me give you a sum I have brought with me, and out of which you can distribute your farewell charities to those poor pensioners of whom you have often spoken to me; and if you will send me a list of their names, my darling, my steward shall visit and relieve them in your absence." So saying, he put a purse into Edith's hands, who took it with a fresh burst of tears.

With these words, the old Earl clasped the wildly weeping girl in a long embrace, and tore himself away. She rushed out, and saw him enter his carriage, to which Arthur, who was in the garden, was assisting him. She heard him say, "God bless and prosper you, Arthur—take care of my Edith;" and then she saw no more, for the Earl drew himself up in a corner of the carriage, and hid his face in his hands.

CHAPTER XII.

"Child no more! I love, and I am woman!"
RICHELIEU.

As soon as the old Earl was fairly off, Edith hastened to her own room to think, to pray, to weep, and then to wash away the traces of her tears, for she had to repair to Mr. Croft's library, to complete some calculations, accounts, and book-keeping (which, as she was an excellent arithmetician, she always managed for him).

Edith longed to be once more in the woods and fields with Arthur, for it was exquisitely fine; but she had promised Mr. Croft to complete all she had undertaken, and Edith never broke her word. Since we saw him last, Mr. Croft has been to Paris, and a French hairdresser had persuaded him to adopt a curly ventilating peruke. It gave him a jaunty, perky air, by no means natural to the staid old attorney; and as he sat in his easy chair by the fire, conning his Murray's Handbook, and glancing approvingly at Edith, his pretty book-keeper, pondering over a total at her own little writing-table, a more cheery home-scene could not have been designed.

By the time Edith had finished her work, Arthur had entered the drawing-room in search of her.

They had agreed, as it was their last day at Rockalpine, to pay farewell visits to some poor cottagers living on the moor. "Duty first, and pleasure afterwards," was Edith's motto; and now, with loving hearts, they wander forth together, bathed in the rich sunset, hand-in-hand, on their errand of mercy,

—silent, but yet happy; for them it was the Spring-time of life—the Dawn of Love—the fairy-land of the heart; and they wanted nothing to make them blest but the dear delight of roaming together through Nature's wild scenery—silent with that silence which is more eloquent than words, and a soft sigh occasionally proclaiming a happiness far deeper than that which translates itself into smiles and words.

Mrs. Croft's eldest son was, as we have said, to be of the continental party, and a young fellow-Etonian, Lord Pontecraft, eldest son of a great Northumbrian nobleman, the Marquis of Dunstanburgh, was also to be of the travellers.

Mrs. Croft's son was a very forward, vulgar young fellow, with a great deal of the "fast man," and the "gent," or rather snob, about him. He affected to be a great admirer (in a patronising sort of manner) of "little Edith," as he was in the habit of calling her; but in his heart he felt a great reverence for Edith Lorraine, as the grand-daughter of an earl—an earl, too, so powerful in his native county as was Rockalpine—and, in all human probability, soon to be the Lady Edith Lorraine, daughter of the Earl of Rockalpine.

At Eton, young Croft had learnt the full value of rank, title, power, hereditary influence, wealth, and position; and very early had he and his worldly mother planned his securing by marriage what had been denied him by birth. But then, on the other hand, Lord Pontecraft showed alarming symptoms of love for Edith, although it had been hoped that one of the Misses Croft would have had power to attract him—for they were very pretty, dressed well, and were highly accomplished. But Edith had that peculiar charm—that something—which no heart of man can resist. It was not merely beauty—in point of beauty, the Misses Croft might have contested the palm with Edith—it was that rare union of grace, expression, sympathy, feeling, humour, fascination, nature, which occasionally *do* form one irresistible whole, and make the woman in whom they centre, the Queen of Hearts, even if endowed with a much smaller share of beauty than that which fell to the share of the pretty delicate Edith.

Both young Croft and Lord Pontecraft were jealous of Arthur. A close league existed between them; they both had very "varmint" propensities; both loved smoking, drinking, betting, racing; both had triumphs to record in the way of clandestine visits to casinos, and conquests far more disgraceful than defeats!

Both were very disagreeable to the delicate taste and refined susceptibilities of Edith Lorraine. But Edith hated to give pain, and often concealed the dislike and disgust she felt, rather than wound the maternal affection (or rather vanity) of Mrs. Croft, who took an intense interest in her son's success as an *élégant*, and was extremely anxious that Lord Pontecraft should find sufficient attraction in the home-circle about to remove abroad, to secure his following them in all their peregrinations.

While the young Lord Pontecraft, and his crony, Croft, were strutting together up and down the broad gravel walks of the grounds of Croft Villa—their glazed hats cocked on one side, their costume nautical, and prepared for the yacht—smoking their cigars, and boasting of their adventures in odious slang, plentifully seasoned with what they called "bounces," "crams," and "wops," the Misses Croft were busy with the milliner, and maid, in devising the most becoming yachting costumes, with a view to captivate Lord Pontecraft; and Mrs. Croft, a great allopathist, was intent upon her medicine-chest, and a glass jar of leeches, travelling companions with whom she could not possibly dispense.

Meanwhile, Arthur and Edith walked on, hand-in-hand, across the fields golden with buttercups, and fragrant with cowslips, over the stiles, across the shallow brooks, through the Black Wood (of such terrible memory in this tale, and which even they, could not pass without a shudder, for they knew its dark story), and came out upon the purple moor.

A poor old cripple now lived in that hovel which had once belonged to Rough Rob and his Irish Mary.

In their long rambles, Arthur and Edith had come upon this poor old cripple, and had more than once helped him with small sums of money, and had taken him tea, sugar, broth, and other nourishing things.

And now they have resolved to pay a last visit to poor old Juke, and to leave with him a share of the sum the Earl has left in Edith's hands to distribute in farewell gifts to her poor pensioners.

The sun was setting as the young lovers crossed the purple, buoyant, and fragrant moor.

"Look! what is this, Arthur?" said Edith, just as they left the Black Wood, stooping down to examine a little feathery bundle of mauve and green and gold, fluttering in the heather.

"A woodpigeon!" said Arthur, "a wounded woodpigeon! Ah, doubtless, one shot by Lord Pontecraft or Roger Croft, when they were out with their guns this morning. See, it is bleeding!"

"Is it much hurt?" said Edith, growing pale. "Oh, the cruel, cruel sport! to wound a bird, is much worse than to kill it."

"I do not think its wing is broken, although it is bleeding," said Arthur. "Shall we try to save it, dear Edith?"

"Of course, Arthur; we could not leave it to die."

"Stop, then," said Arthur, "I will make a sort of basket of heather for it, and we will carry it home."

"And I," said Edith, "will bind up its wing with my handkerchief; for I think, in fluttering as it does, it keeps the wound open."

Arthur, who had helping hands, soon wove some branches of heather into a sort of nest or basket, and Edith adroitly bound the injured wing, and then she lifted the poor woodpigeon into the nest, covered it over with Arthur's pocket-handkerchief, and walked on with it towards the hovel on the moor.

Arthur and Edith had proceeded as far as an old thorn, which stretched its gnome-like and distorted trunk across their path, and which at this season of the year was covered with brilliant verdure and luxuriant tufts of snow-white blossom, of most nutty fragrance, when, from behind its shelter, a gipsy, in a dark red cloak, with a hood, from beneath which blazed a pair of fierce black eyes, suddenly came forth and confronted them.

Both Arthur and Edith had occasionally seen this weird woman before.

She was held in great awe, and even dread, in that part of the country. She was a genuine gipsy, and Superstition endowed her with the power of telling fortunes, foretelling events, casting evil eyes, blighting, banning, and doing every possible evil, if offended, but often proving a good and valuable friend where she "took to people," as the country folk had it. She was a singularly powerful, picturesque, and remarkable woman; and her elf locks of raven black hair, large jetty eyes, her very brown skin, scarlet lips, and glittering white teeth, had a sort of wild beauty and captivation about them.

"Cross my hand with silver, young gentleman," she said, in the professional whine of her tribe, "and I'll tell you your lucky fortune."

"No, I thank you, Madge," said Arthur, "I had rather not know it."

"Well," said Madge, "there's that in it would scare the bravest."

"Oh, don't say that, good Madge!" said Edith, turning pale.

"Never fear, pretty lady," said Madge; "a stout heart in his breast, and a true maid by his side, will help him through. But let me examine your palm, young gentleman, and I'll tell you more, and may be much that it concerned you to know."

"Do, Arthur, let Madge look at your hand," said Edith, giving the gipsy half-a-crown.

And Arthur laughingly agreed, for he never refused a request of Edith's.

"You are not what you seem," said the gipsy.

"Am I better or worse than I seem, Madge?" laughed Arthur.

"Both! You've in your veins some of the noblest blood in the land; and straight before you in your path of life, a coronet and a castle await you."

Edith started; the gipsy's prophecy tallied with that of the old earl.

"What! am I to gain distinction at the bar, Madge?" said Arthur; "am I to be a judge—a law lord?"

"No; the coronet I mean is yours by right of birth."

"Ah! you're out there, Madge, at any rate," said Arthur.

"Edith Lorraine!" said the gipsy, "when it comes to pass—when he is the recognised heir of a noble house, and sits in his coronet and ermine in the House of Lords—remember Madge the gipsy foretold the event."

"Shall I be happy in love, Madge?" said Arthur.

"'The course of true love never *did* run smooth,'" said Madge; "but constancy on both sides will conquer at last. 'Faint heart never won fair lady.' See that yours faints not. You'll have crosses and foes, and 'whispering tongues, that poison truth,' will be busy between you and about you; but trust each other; be true, be faithful; and when you take your seat in the House of Peers in coronet and ermine, young man, a countess's coronet shall grace her brow, and a peeress's robes shall hang about her form. And now listen; you are bound for Rough Rob's hovel on the moor; turn back your footsteps—go not thither."

"But we promised to go," said Edith.

"Rash promises are better broken than kept, pretty lady," said the gipsy. "It is late—it is getting dark—hasten back to the villa."

She ceased, and hurried off in the direction of the village.

" Shall we obey her?" said Edith.

"I should say no, dear Edith," said Arthur; "I have no fear—not I; let us hasten on. These gipsies often pretend there is peril in order to show their power. Besides, what does she know of our Past, Present, or Future? She must be a mere pretender—an impostor. Did you hear her nonsense about noble blood in my veins, and a coronet and a castle in my path of life? I quite see through that; she has heard that Pontecraft is here. These gipsies trade on gossip. She fancied I was Pontecraft, and with that idea, of course a coronet and a castle might well be in my path of life, and noble blood in my veins. She's done for herself, in my opinion, by such rubbish as that. So come, dear Edith, come!"

CHAPTER XIII.

> "Some flowers of Eden we still inherit,
> But the trail of the serpent is over them all."
>
> MOORE.

HAND-IN-HAND the young lovers glided on, through bowers of fragrance and verdure, and "over yellow meads of Asphodel."

Lovely and innocent as the first pair, ere Sin found his way into the groves of Eden, they were as loving and as happy too.

There was something so noble, so manly, so protecting in Arthur's tall well-knit form, and in the frank, handsome face, rather sun-burnt (for Arthur was no Sybarite), that was bent down to her clear, upraised eyes with looks of such confiding, such unutterable love. The birds were singing as if to welcome them; the flowers seemed to spring up to deck their path; the slanting rays of the setting sun were reflected in Arthur's dark eyes and on Edith's chestnut hair as they glided on.

Since the time when Rough Rob had inhabited the cottage on the moor, great changes had taken place; a branch railway (concealed by a ridge of hills) passed at no great distance; and a cottage, belonging to one of the railway officials, had been built, about ten minutes' walk from Rough Rob's old abode. But no trace of this residence was to be seen.

The place looked, indeed, as wild, desolate, and lonely as it had done ten years before.

Edith and Arthur then proceeded to the hovel, and there fulfilled their promise and performed their errand of mercy.

The cripple was not alone—three down-looking, savage, ragged men, of muscular frames and murderous countenances, were smoking in his room; and Edith, as she took out the purse in which was the sum her grandfather had given her for her farewell charities, shuddered to see the eyes of these men exchange rapid glances, and then fasten with an evil and rapacious glitter on the purse in her hand. Shortly after this they rose, and with a muttered good night took their leave.

The cripple, old Juke, was full of thanks and benedictions; but there was something that struck both Edith and Arthur as canting, hurried, and unreal in what he said. He was Irish, and so were the stalwart fellows smoking, who had lounged off, and who had certainly been drinking, for a strong smell of whiskey pervaded the hovel. Juke invoked "ivery saint in the calendar to bliss his binifactors" (as he called Edith and Arthur), and implored the "blissed Virgin to make their bed the night!" But he did not look them in the face as he spoke; and they were very glad to leave the close hovel, that smelt so strongly of smoke and spirits, and to breathe again the fragrance of the purple heather and the nutty-scented thorns.

"I am so glad to be out of that hovel, Arthur," said Edith. "I did not much like old Juke to-day, nor those savage-looking men."

"Nor I," said Arthur; "let us get back as fast as we can, Edith."

Edith, clinging to Arthur's arm, hurried on with him, and insisted on carrying the handkerchief in which the wounded pigeon and his impromptu nest were tied up. They have reached the old thorn where they had met Madge, and Edith paused for a moment to take breath.

"I wonder," said Arthur, "where those three ill-looking fellows went. I am certain they were ruffians."

He had scarcely uttered those words, when

a blow with a heavy stick on the back of his head made him turn round, and he then perceived that the three ill-looking fellows who had left Juke's hovel before them, and who had been lying in wait for them behind the old thorn, were upon them.

Wildly poor Edith screamed, and brutally one of the men pressed his rough, black hand upon her mouth to silence her.

At the sight of this outrage, Arthur, his blood on fire, wrenched the bludgeon from the hand of the wretch who had assaulted him, and with a well-aimed blow brought Edith's assailant to the ground. But the contest was an unequal one. The two other villains fell upon Arthur, who, in spite of a valiant resistance, was overpowered, stunned, and forced to the ground, which was soon bathed in his blood. Edith's pockets were rifled of her purse, and every valuable she possessed was taken from her; while she, paralysed with alarm at Arthur's state, sank fainting by his side.

After robbing Arthur of his watch and his purse, the villains made their escape; and it was not till a quarter of an hour later that a young railway official, on his way to his mother's cottage, came suddenly upon the ghastly spectacle of Arthur, stunned and bleeding, on the moor, and Edith in a dead swoon, her head on his breast.

The young man lifted the light form of Edith Lorraine in his arms, and bore her, still insensible, along the pathway across the moor, and into the neat little parlour, where his mother and sisters were awaiting him. He, at the same time, despatched two labouring men, who had been working in the garden, and were waiting for their day's wages from him, with a hurdle, whereon to place the wounded Arthur. By this time it was almost dark.

Great was the surprise and alarm of Mrs.

Parker, the official's neat, tidy mother, and of his two pretty sisters, when Dick came in, bearing in his arms the apparently lifeless form of Edith.

Her hat had fallen off as he entered, and her long, glossy, auburn hair fell in dishevelled beauty over his arm. Her sweet face was perfect in its marble beauty; but Mrs. Parker, who knew Death well, for out of eight children she had but three left, saw that the "fell serpeant's" unmistakeable mark was not on that brow, and said to her son,

"She's only fainted, Dick, and my camphor julep will soon bring her too."

Patty Parker, the eldest sister, picked up Edith's hat, and hastened to her assistance, adding her eager queries to those of her mother and her sister Jessy. But Dick had no time to enter into particulars. He only said,

"Stand out of the way, that I may lay her

on a bed; and do you, mother dear, and you, my sisters, try to revive her. I think with you, mother, that she has only fainted. I will be back directly."

So saying, he carried Edith into an inner room, and placed her on a bed and then darted back to the spot where he had left Arthur, to assist the labourers in bringing the wounded youth to his mother's cottage.

Dick Parker, the railway guard, arrived at the spot where he had left Arthur in time to superintend his removal to the cottage. Gently and carefully the wounded youth was placed on a hurdle, the wood-pigeon, whose terrified flutter in its heather nest, and under the silk pocket-handkerchief, had attracted kind Dick Parker's notice, being carried by himself.

Dick Parker was a fine, handsome young fellow, with "a heart that could feel for another," even if that other were only a wounded wood-pigeon; and very tenderly the young man carried the poor bird, and very warmly was the pretty flutterer welcomed and caressed by the two neat blooming girls, his sisters.

Edith had recovered from her swoon by the time Arthur was brought in, and at the sound of men's voices she sprang from the bed on which she had been placed, and hurried into the little parlour, calling aloud on her "Arthur!—her dear, dear Arthur!"

Mrs. Parker, who had seen, as we have said, a great deal of sickness and death, and was not only a capital nurse, but, in her own simple ways a very clever surgeon, prepared to do her best for Arthur, until the village doctor, for whom she had sent, could reach the spot.

Arthur was stunned and faint from loss of blood, but not seriously nor dangerously hurt. The colour returned to Edith's lips and cheeks when Mrs. Parker assured her of this; and, with singular presence of mind and dexterity, she helped the good, motherly woman to wash the blood from Arthur's pale face, to cut away the clotted clusters of hair from the wound, to bind it up, and to administer some simple restoratives, which soon enabled him (with a faint smile of recognition) to extend his hand to Edith, who, her heart and soul in her eager eyes, was kneeling by his side.

"He will do very well, my dear young lady," said Mrs. Parker; "let us be thankful, bad as it is, that it is no worse."

"Now that I feel a little easier in my mind," said Edith, "I will tell you how this came to pass, and who and what we are."

She then, as simply and succinctly as possible, related the adventures of herself and Arthur, from the time of their meeting with the gipsy Madge to that of the savage attack made upon them by the three ruffians who had hidden up behind the thorn, evidently to await their coming.

"I never had any opinion of old Juke myself," said Mrs. Parker, "and so I've told Dick scores of times. He's too full of blarney for me, and he has always some ill-looking fellows hanging about his wretched hovel. However, the police will now be set to work, and I hope these ruffians will be sent out of the country. But don't you think, miss, we'd better contrive to let your friends know of the accident?"

At this moment one of the labourers returned, saying that Dr. Fussell would be there as soon as possible; and, after he had imbibed a pint of beer, this same man was despatched to Croft Villa to apprise Mr. and Mrs. Croft of what had happened.

Dr. Fussell soon made his appearance. He was a little, red-faced, bright-eyed, bald-headed man in top boots; he was a clever, skilful surgeon, and was full of gossip and jokes—a very gallant old fellow, a great admirer of beauty, rather a flirt, but extremely kind to the poor, often giving them out of his own kitchen and pocket that help which the more stingy guardians denied them. He was always in disgrace with the "Board" for the expenses to which his benevolence put them; and he had a running joke, which he cracked at all meetings of the guardians, about the feeling and sympathy to be expected from a *board*.

The gay widows and the prim spinsters of Alnwick and Rockalpine had long and vainly set their caps at Dr. Fussell. He attended their parties when he could, liked a rubber and a nice little hot supper at Christmas, was ready as a partner in Sir Roger de Coverley, but *never offered his hand for more than one dance*.

There was a very wealthy old spinster, who

lived at a dull place called Moor House, and who was a prey to countless diseases, both real and imaginary. Her name was Miss Trumpington—the Honourable Melissa Trumpington. She was so very fond of the little gallant, bright, jocose, and clever doctor, who had always so much gossip wherewith to amuse her, that many people believed she would marry him. She had a pretty, pale, patient companion, a very distant relative, who had been in close attendance upon her from sixteen to thirty-two, and for whom she was expected to providé; but although she *had* a heart disease, which might at any moment carry her off, she did not appear to have made any will or in any manner to have provided for Miriam Moss.

Dr. Fussell undertook the delicate task of reminding the Hon. Miss Trumpington of the destitution that awaited poor Miss Moss if unprovided for in her patroness's will.

Miss Trumpington very haughtily replied, that she was quite competent to the management of her own affairs, and wanted no hints from anyone—that if Miss Moss was not satisfied she was at full liberty to go; and there the subject ended. Dr. Fussell never alluded to it again, and for a few days Miss Trumpington did not send for him. But ere long some sharp bodily pains conquered pride, and he was reinstated. He was on his way to Moor House when the labourer met with him, only he had to call first at a cottage where a poor man, who, in chopping wood, had cut an artery, would have bled to death but for his timely aid.

Dr. Fussell started when he recognised Edith Lorraine in the young lady kneeling by the wounded youth's side. Edith had more than once been under his care. Arthur, too, though generally so healthy, had been his patient in the case of two or three childish maladies. Both were favourites with the good little doctor.

"Ah! fair Edith of the swan neck!" he said, offering his warm hand. "What, bending over Harold? Not slain, I hope? No, no! Never say die! Come, how are we now?" and he sat down by Arthur's side, took his hand with a professional air, and felt his pulse. "Very low and fluttering," he said; "Mrs. Parker, have we a little good brandy in our cupboard?"

"Yes, sir; I have some French brandy."

"Very good. Now let's have some boiling water, and a glass, and some lump sugar. This spirit, fair Edith, which does so much evil, does sometimes a great deal of good. It has often brought Sin and Death into the world, but sometimes the life of a dear one is owing to its potency. Now then, here we are. Take a sip yourself, fair Edith. You need it, for you are much shaken, and we know who will think the cordial all the sweeter, if those pretty lips touch it :—

> 'But leave a kiss within the cup,
> And I'll not ask for wine,'"

he sang, in a little, squeaky falsetto.

Arthur, to whose lips Dr. Fussell placed the glass, drank, and as he did so his colour returned, he opened his eyes, he smiled kindly on the cheery little Fussell, and said in a faint voice,

"I don't think I'm much hurt, Doctor. Do tell Edith so—she's frightened to death."

"Hurt! no, not a bit of it! She's not frightened; not she. Pretty girls like a little blood shed in their cause. There isn't a woman in the world, high or low, who doesn't like a young fellow all the better if he's got a bloody costard in her service. There, now, take another pull at this mixture here," and he poured some into two other glasses. "Now then, Edith fair; now then, Prince Arthur;

now then, Dr. Fussell—a long pull and a strong pull and a pull all together! There now, we're twice the men we were. Mrs. Parker, Dick, my boy, and you, Jessie and Patty, come and try this prescription; you all look frightened to death."

After every one had partaken of the brandy and water, and Arthur had held out his hand to Edith, who took it unconsoious of aught but the rapture of seeing him restored to life and to her, the little Doctor said,

"And now to business. Now we must see what's the extent of the damage. Mrs. Parker, you'll be my best assistant here; hold a light, if you please. It's an ugly cut, and a deep one; but it's doing well, as well as can be expected! Very neatly dressed, indeed! Now, have you a bed, my good Mrs. Parker, which you can spare for our young Squire here? Darkness, quiet, and a composing draught, that's all we can do for him; and all we have to exact from our womankind is a miracle—but Love does work miracles—namely, Silence! They *must* hold their tongues, for when once the patient has taken this anodyne, all will depend on rest—entire rest. There's a little tendency to fever; and that's the only thing we have to fear. Show me the bed he can have."

Mrs. Parker led the little Doctor into the inner room, and showed him the bed on which Edith had been placed.

"The very thing. Now then, young ladies, if you will leave the field, we'll get our wounded hero to bed; and when he's quite comfortable, I'll come upstairs and ask Edith fair to give me a brief account of the 'moving accident by flood and field' that led to this disaster."

Arthur, upon this, held out his hand for Edith's, which he pressed to his lips, and with a mutual "good night" and "Heaven bless you!" they parted.

In about half an hour the little Doctor and Mrs. Parker came upstairs to hear from Edith that account of the disaster which she had already given to the Parkers. While she related it, a carriage drove up to the door, and, pale and trembling, Mr. Croft was ushered up to them.

A little of the Doctor's magic brew did him a world of good. He agreed not to disturb Arthur; and he consented to Edith's passionate wish to remain where she was that night, Jessy having offered to give up her little bed to the young lady, and to lie with her mother and sister.

Mr. Croft then left the cottage, with the comfortable assurance on the part of the little Doctor, that in all probability Arthur would be well enough to return to the Villa the next day.

CHAPTER XIV.

"Thus conscience doth make cowards of us all."
SHAKESPEARE.

WHILE the worldly *parvenue*, Lady Hauteville, is preparing with such pride and triumph for Augusta's marriage with the Earl of Richlands, and while Edith—whom in her hard heart she has doomed to the perpetual spinsterhood that so often awaits a cripple—is enjoying all that happiness that Love and Youth can bestow on Innocence, there were hearts in which the proud Lorraine blood was chilled by dread, or fevered with anguish and despair. Lord Hauteville, in spite of his success in public life, in spite of Popularity,

Reputation, Office, could never shake from his soul that nightmare, the consciousness of Crime, and that ever-haunting, chilling terror that attends the dread of Detection.

Rough Rob and his Mary were in Canada; but things did not go well with them there, not any better than they had done in Australia. Mike O'Rourke, from Mary's account, was a rash speculator and an inexperienced farmer, and had led them to the verge of ruin. Mary was the scribe of the party, and *would* write to Lord Hauteville, although the sight of her handwriting, and her square letters, and her thimble seal, caused him an ague of fear and anguish, and though he sent large sums to keep Rough Rob abroad; for he was haunted by an impression, so vivid as to seem almost a *pressentiment*, that if once Rough Rob were taken and tried, the long-hidden and terrible truth would come to light.

Augusta, on her side, could not stifle with

wedding finery the yearnings of a young and not unfeeling heart. She dreaded to be alone —she dreaded to think; she studiously avoided all *tête-à-têtes* with her intended, the wigged, padded, rouged old Earl, with his glittering false teeth, so out of keeping with the thin blue lips of age; his blackened eyebrows and whiskers, so harsh and unnatural when contrasted with the wrinkled parchment of his cheeks and brow, and which the silvery locks of age would have softened; and his stiff gait, so ill suited to his assumed juvenility.

Alas! poor shrinking bride elect! If thou so dreadest a few minutes alone with thy lord elect, how wilt thou endure the close intimacy, the forced companionship, of wedded life—the unbroken seclusion of that honeymoon which will so soon tear thee from all but him at whose tottering steps and squeaky falsetto thy cheek grows pale, and the young blood dancing in thy veins grows icy cold? Happier—oh! ten thousand times—beautiful and stately Augusta! bride elect of an Earl! is little Edith (the carroty cripple). Carroty cripple, indeed! why, Hebe might envy the golden auburn of her rippled tresses, and Psyche could ask no form more perfect and more sylphlike. Yes, ten thousand times happier is Edith, with her young, adoring, but unacknowledged lover by her side, though he *is* the grandson of Attorney Croft, adopted out of charity, and, in the world's opinion, as far beneath thee as Attorney Croft is beneath the great Lord Hauteville, the popular orator, the Cabinet Minister, the man whose reputation is without a stain or blemish, and who, if there *were* an order of Virtue and Merit, would be a Knight Grand Cross of that Order, and wear its priceless star on the breast of—a fratricide!

In about a week from the time of the

assault and robbery on the moor, Arthur was sufficiently recovered to embark on board Mr. Croft's yacht, the *Water Lily*, in company with the happy party going abroad for the first time.

The police had made every possible effort to discover and apprehend the ruffians who had committed the assault and theft; but all their endeavours proved abortive. Old Juke had left his hovel, and was gone none knew whither; and thus one great chance of detection was lost.

A reward of a hundred pounds was offered by the Earl, and another to the same amount by the parish authorities, for the apprehension of the culprits; but in vain. Our party embarked without any progress having been made in the detection of the ruffians.

Edith spent the last day of her sojourn in England at Rockalpine Castle, with her grandfather. It was a happy day, for his love and tenderness were proportioned to the great boon which he felt he owed to his little Edith.

The delay in the departure of Mrs. Croft and her party enabled the former to receive before she embarked the wedding-cards of the Countess of Richlands. Yes, Augusta had consoled the forsaken suitor of her sister; the sacrifice was complete. She had wedded her eighteen summers to the Earl's sixty-eight winters; and so quietly had it all been managed, that the London world of fashion was taken quite by surprise; and before Slander, Gossip, and Ridicule could make a feast out of their engagement, Interest silenced all three; for Augusta was a Countess, and the Countess's robes covered up all the vanity, avarice, and ambition of such a match.

Lady Hauteville, although for a time her occupation was gone, as she had no daughter to marry, continued in town for the remainder of the season, she so thoroughly enjoyed the envy, malice, and discomfiture of high-born matrons, with daughters of many seasons still on hand.

The young Countess had promised that her absence should not extend beyond the honey-moon, and then she was to return to town, be again presented as a bride—the Countess of Richlands—to glitter at the Birthday Drawing-room, give some superb dinners and *soirées*, and a *fête* and ball hitherto unapproached for magnificence, at Richlands House, Park Lane, and to display her diamonds and her *trousseau* before admiring or envying eyes, to the de-light of Lady Hauteville, who scarcely ever now gave a thought to her once favourite Georgina, or to "that poor little carroty cripple, Edith," so completely was she ab-sorbed in the contemplation of the splendid match her Augusta had made.

However, Lady Hauteville, who had the

wit "to assume a virtue, if she had it not," had written a very civil letter to Mrs. Croft, and a few slanting affectionate lines to Edith. To the former she said :—

"MY DEAREST MRS. CROFT,—You will receive by this post the wedding-cards of my sweet Augusta, now the Countess of Richlands. The dear girl in her first season, and, as you know, only eighteen, has carried off a prize for which high-born and fashionable mothers and daughters have long contended in vain. In the midst of her tumultuous happiness she did not forget to ask me to send her cards and those of her Richlands to you and our poor little suffering Edith; and she rejoiced with me to hear that our afflicted darling has the chance of change of air and scene, and that, owing to your maternal care, she is in a state in some degree to enjoy the tour you propose to make. Lord Hauteville is more than ever absorbed by politics, and the duties entailed on him by office; but he shares with me in the comfort we feel in our Augusta's happy marriage, which, indeed, is the more to be rejoiced at, as our eldest darling, in marrying a foreign nobleman, consulted her own taste, not ours, and is, I fear, in a great measure lost to us.

"I much wish I could have visited Rockalpine before this, to have embraced my darling Edith, and to have thanked you, her second mother, for all your care; but since his brother's dreadful death, Lord Hauteville has never been happy at Rockalpine, and never visits the place, unless when duty to his father compels him to do so.

"You said in your last that you perceive no change in the Earl, my father-in-law. What a wonderful thing that, at his age, he should be so hale and strong! Northumbrians are like Scotchmen—they live for ever.

"Adieu, my dearest Mrs. Croft. Embrace my poor Edith for me, and believe me ever

"Yours most faithfully,

"GEORGINA HAUTEVILLE."

To Edith, her mother wrote:—

"MY DEAREST EDITH,—I am grieved to the soul at not being able to see you, and clasp you to my heart, before you set out on the delightful tour which dear Mrs. Croft has so charmingly contrived for you. I am enchanted to hear from her, my poor love, that you are in all respects stronger and better in health than you were when I last saw you. Perhaps when you return from this long sojourn on the Continent, you will be grown so much I shall hardly recognise you. I hope at that time to introduce you to your new brother-in-law—the Earl of Richlands. I am certain you will like him, he is so kind! Augusta is a very fortunate girl.

"Adieu, my darling Edith. May all good angels watch over you, by sea and by land, prays

"Your devoted mother,

"GEORGINA HAUTEVILLE."

Mrs. Croft was very proud of such an affectionate and communicative letter as that she had received from Lady Hauteville. Great as was the distance *now* between the wife of Lawyer Croft and Lady Hauteville, the time had been, before Sir John Armstrong became a baronet and a millionaire, when Miss Armstrong and Miss Clutterbuck had attended the same drawing and dancing-schools at Alnwick, and had been rival beauties at the dancing-master's ball. And now, her father's success in life, and her own ambition, had raised the one so far above the other, that her slightest notice was an honour that could not be too highly appreciated.

And what has become of the rash, the misguided, the unhappy Georgina? Has the veil fallen from her eyes? Has the spell of passion outlasted the honeymoon? Alas! it seldom does so. Nor is Georgina's case an exception to the general rule.

Romeo di Roccabella has already succeeded, by the aid and advice of some crafty pettifoggers, in getting a considerable part of Georgina's twenty thousand pounds advanced—that is to say, he has sold the reversion to a very Shylock, and he has insured her life for double the amount; and, armed with the money obtained by the sale of her reversion, he has repaired to the German Spas to endeavour to quadruple it, for Romeo di Roccabella is a desperate gamester.

He has all a gamester's moody, fitful tempers. He has gained his object—the money is his! What little passion or fleeting fancy he had for the wretched victim of his cupidity is quite sated. She is in his way; she is an encumbrance, an expense, a reproach! She is discontented, too, unhappy, jealous, watchful.

Alone during the long days and the sleepless nights, which he spends at the gaming-tables, how bitterly the poor young wife repents of that one false step! How she pines for pardon, and for restoration to her home and her sister!

In vain, in vain! All the letters she writes are returned unopened; and Romeo di Roccabella, exasperated at her despair, her tears, her misery, commands her, on peril of his dire resentment, to write no more! To add to her wretchedness, her health and strength fail her, her beauty vanishes like a dream. A sickness as unto death constantly oppresses her, making life a burthen; she wastes to a shadow, and hopes—poor wretch!—she *hopes* she is about to die!

Her Romeo, when she tells him so, does not weep; through the affected concern of his false face, the miserable wife detects a glitter of joy in his eye, and a half smile on his moustachioed lip. However, he insists on her having advice, and the opinion of the first physician in Homburg.

Georgina watched him closely while the doctor expressed his opinion, and the cloud that darkened his brow cast its cold shadow on her sinking heart. The doctor, an old *bon vivant*, and a laughing philosopher, rubbed his hands, chuckled, and congratulated the Count and the Countess, saying, "You'll be worse before you're better, my dear Countess; it's life, not death, that causes all these symptoms. In due time a little stranger will atone for all these sufferings."

Unhappy Georgina! there is no joy, no sympathy, in his eye, and yet he is thy husband—he is the father of the child to be born of thee! To him the news is gall and wormwood. He does not clasp thee to his heart, and bless and cheer thee. He leaves thee alone in thy new and perplexing position; but even *he* cannot chill the glow with which woman first learns that she is to be a mother! No! he cannot rob thee of that strange, mystic rapture! And he sees thee, with an evil, mocking eye, taking care of thy feeble health for the sake of the unborn—he, who so wishes that death would claim both the branch and the fruit, for he has insured thy young life for twenty thousand pounds!

CHAPTER XV.

"O'er the glad waters of the dark blue sea,
Our hearts as boundless and our souls as free;
Where'er the winds can waft, the billows roam,
Survey our empire, and behold our home."

BYRON.

MR. CROFT, although his wife had induced him to purchase that splendid yacht, the *Water Lily*, was by no means nautically disposed. He, as he said, did not know a rope of the ship, and was a wretched sailor; but he was far too sensible to pretend to be what he was not, or to undertake what he could not achieve, particularly when his doing so would have endangered the lives of others. He wisely hired a thoroughly competent and experienced captain and crew; and soon after embarkation, both he and Mrs. Croft, their daughters, Roger Croft, and the young Lord, were all lying on their backs in their berths, in all the depressing, unbearable agonies of sea-sickness, all wishing for nothing but to be once again on *terra firma;* all resolving, that if ever such rapture were theirs, nothing would ever again induce them to enter a yacht, or to do anything in that way, but crossing back to England on a very calm summer day, *viâ* Calais and Dover.

However, the voyage, which was such misery to all the rest of the party, was enchantment to Edith and Arthur. They were not in the least ill; on the contrary, they were in unusual health and spirits (as those who are not afflicted with sickness always are when at sea). The wood-pigeon, now quite recovered and very tame, was their constant companion, and was a pet with all on deck.

The colours of the rainbow touched with gold shone in the sun, as its rays lighted the bird's neck, and its coo had a melancholy, not at all unwelcome to the ear of Love.

They were always together, were Edith and Arthur. At early morn they loved to see the sun rise in his glory and illumine the ocean; at noonday they reposed side by side in the shade, Arthur reading some enchanting sea-novel of Marryat's or Cooper's aloud to Edith. When it was calm they were happy in the soothing repose of the soft undulation; when the breeze freshened they loved to ride the crested waves, and be now wafted on high, now plunged below, but always together.

Edith would fain have sacrificed herself and the dear delights of the deck to the horrors of the cabins and berths of the sufferers below. But their tempers were so soured by their long suffering, and they so envied her the enjoyment of what was such purgatory to them, that she met with no encouragement to prolong or renew her visits. Mrs. Croft and her daughters, never very amiable, were now all spleen, lamentation, and unjust reproach. Arthur did not fare much better in his attempts to comfort Mr. Croft, Lord Pontefract, and Roger Croft. The former was really very ill; the two latter kept up the sea-sickness by vain attempts to smoke, to drink champagne and brown stout; and Arthur could scarcely be expected to give up Edith, and the open sea, the fresh air, and the beautiful sky, for the thankless, jeering, sulky victims of tobacco, brown stout, and champagne. But at length the paradise of Edith and Arthur, and the purgatory of all the others, came to a close.

They landed one fine evening at Elsinore, in Denmark; and, in a few days, all the sufferers, including Mr. Croft, were able to enjoy the beauty of a spot so associated in every English mind with Shakespeare and his great "masterpiece, Hamlet."

The Misses Croft began now to set their caps, or rather their pork-pie hats, in earnest at the young Lord; and young Croft disgusted the young Danish ladies by strutting about, his cigar in his mouth, his hands in his pockets, staring them out of countenance. One day, the eldest Miss Croft, who began to despair of making any impression on the young Lord, asked Edith and Arthur to accompany her on a visit to some ruins of great interest a few miles off. She had met unexpectedly at Elsinore (indeed at Hamlet's tomb) with a gentleman who had paid her a good deal of attention during a visit to an aunt in London.

This person, a Mr. Horton, was a young barrister, rather sneering and jeering, but well-dressed, with moustaches, a good figure, and a handsome face, although the expression was sinister and rather sly. Still Miss Croft, who was very weary of the thankless task of courting the young Lord, was very glad to meet with any one at all disposed to court her, and she hoped in this excursion to bring him to the point.

Mr. Horton and Arthur were to row Edith and Miss Croft to the ruin. Mrs. Croft and the rest were to go in a carriage, and meet them at the old castle with luncheon, &c., &c. It was a lovely day; the skies were of a deep turquoise blue, the water, smooth as glass, was rich in water-lilies and lotuses, and the banks were so beautifully enamelled with wild flowers, that at Edith's request the boat was put in, and they landed, that the ladies might gather the wild hyacinths and the wood strawberries with which the place abounded.

Miss Croft and Mr. Horton, hanging back, did not seem disposed to leave the fairy spot; but Arthur, who had promised Mrs. Croft not to keep the party waiting for luncheon, took Edith by the hand to help her into the boat. And as he stood, with his oar in one hand, and the other clasping Edith's to help her into the boat, his animated face looking up into hers, and she blushing beneath his ardent gaze, her auburn hair braided back under her little turban hat, her slender form arrayed in a simple white muslin dress, with pearl buttons, and a black silk mantilla on her low, graceful shoulders, you might have sought the world over, without finding a more interesting or a handsomer pair.

But though Edith was so pretty and so graceful, and Arthur was so handsome and so noble a youth, it was the love-light in their eyes, and the "celestial rosy red, love's proper hue," on their blushing cheeks, that gave such a magic charm to both of them, and made them form such a contrast to the pale, calculating, mercenary coquette, and the interested French-looking fortune-hunter, a few steps behind them, and who were making that an opportunity for a mercantile barter, which to Edith and Arthur was an ambrosial ecstasy, a dream of happiness, perhaps too sweet to last, a foretaste of Elysium—the enjoyment of Nature's loveliest haunts in the presence of the adored one.

CHAPTER XVI.

> " She was Italy's daughter, I knew by her eye,
> For it wore the dark hue of her own native sky."

THERE is so strong a moral lesson conveyed by the fate of the unfortunate Georgina, Contessa di Roccabella, that we will leave, for a short space, our Edith and her Arthur, the real hero and heroine of our tale, to trace in Georgina's career the consequences of one false step, and the tragic results of secrecy in love affairs, clandestine correspondence, and, worst of all, their natural result—elopement.

Foreign alliances may turn out well—they have often done so; but then the Chevalier,

Baron, Count, Marquis, Duke, or Prince—(for titles are rife on the Continent, and many of them are of little value or dignity)—should be properly introduced and well known in English society, and to the parents of the object of his choice. His character should be studied closely, his resources well ascertained, and his habits and former mode of life thoroughly sifted. With these precautions, a foreign alliance, may, where there is strong attachment on both sides, and competence, and sympathy in religious opinions, be a very happy one.

But what can we expect when a showy, handsome, mysterious foreigner forms a clandestine acquaintance and a secret intimacy with a young English girl of family and fortune, and works upon her passionate folly and juvenile romance to induce her to elope with him? Let those, then, who, like Georgina, are enamoured cf dark-eyed, moustachioed foreigners, with their captivating guitars, and their graceful mantles, remember that a cloak more frequently conceals a rent than a star.

For some little time after his marriage, of course, Romeo di Roccabella both felt and acted like a lover. Georgina was a perfect specimen of that tall, aristocratic, fair, blue-eyed, blonde beauty, so dear and so new to the sons of the South. Even Di Roccabella, villain and ruffian as he really was, could not but respond to the graceful and romantic fondness of so fair a creature, who had sacrificed a princely fortune, and an English Countess's coronet and fortune, to him; and who so readily and so unsuspectingly agreed to all and everything that he proposed with regard to the fortune left her by her grandfather. Her signature and her consent were necessary both to his selling this reversion and to his insuring her life.

His great objects in marrying her had been

to do both; and it is remarkable that, by the advice and with the help of an English attorney (one Samuel Skuttel), he insured his wife's life to a considerable amount—larger, indeed, than the sum which he had obtained. With the money for which he sold her reversion, he, as the reader knows, hastened to the German Spas, intent on carrying out several schemes for "breaking the banks;" and by degrees, as Georgina's novelty wore off, and she had nothing more to withhold or to grant in regard to money, the Count grew first negligent and cold, and finally rude, cruel, and abusive.

We have said that the wretched Georgina was likely, in due time, to become a mother; and the knowledge of this fact, which filled her heart with such new and delicious sensations, that they almost atoned to her for her Romeo's indifference and cruelty, excited in him no feeling but one of impatience at what he looked upon as a nuisance and a bore, while anger raged within him at the thought of the inevitable expense.

A succession of heavy losses compelled the Count to leave Homburg. He had not patience and temper to be a successful gambler; and he sternly desired Georgina to prepare to go with him to an old castle, the seat of his ancestors, in a wild, remote part of Sicily (on the sea-coast). There, he told her, the heir to the House di Roccabella must, in all probability, be born. It did not seem to occur to him that such a spot might boast neither doctor, nurse, nor any comforts requisite for the unfortunate Countess's safety and solace. Alas! she was too much afraid of him to object.

Thither, then, they went, and thither came, soon after, and by degrees, numbers of dark, fierce-looking moustachioed Italians—who lounged about all day, idling, smoking, and playing cards, and who often did what was far more objectionable, for they tried with their glittering black eyes and their rich Italian voices, which they accompanied with their guitars, to convey to the miserable young wife's mind that they thought her very lovely, and that, at the slightest encouragement, they would be at her feet.

Often for days and nights together Georgina neither saw nor heard of her husband and these his "*free* companions;" and she knew that sometimes they were out on excursions by land, and sometimes by sea; that they met with perilous adventures, of which her slender knowledge of Italian (as taught in England) prevented her understanding the object or the nature, but which even *she* began to suspect had some deeper, darker motive than visits of civility to the nobility of the country, to which her husband haughtily and rather sneeringly attributed them. It is quite certain that these visits were never returned. No Sicilian lords and ladies ever entered the Castello di Roccabella.

The castle was a very large, gloomy building, partly in ruins, and so close to the sea that, in stormy weather, the cellars, and even the marble entrance-hall, had been flooded more than once. The Countess's apartments were on the first floor: they looked on the open sea and the blue skies of Sicily. There were some remains of former grandeur about them, but not one iota of comfort, according to our English notions. The windows had no shutters, and the stone arches of the corridors were open to the air. The fireplaces were like caverns, and, looking up through the broad chimneys, you could see the blue sky. The floors were paved; the stairs were of marble. There were no carpets anywhere but in the countess's bed-room and drawing-room, and those only squares of old tapestry in the middle of the rooms.

Poor Georgina had no English maid with her; in fact, an English maid would have died of discomfort, *ennui*, and despair in such a place. When first she arrived there, an old witch-like woman had the care of the castle, and did all that was not done by wild-looking, banditti-like men in attendance on the Count and his followers.

But when the Contessa's increasing delicacy of health rendered some additional female attendance necessary, and the approach of an heir demanded that it should be some one who could ply her needle in the cause, old Perpetua recommended that her orphan granddaughter, who had been taught needlework at the nearest convent, and who had been in good service besides, should be hired to wait on the Contessa.

Accordingly, Jocunda was introduced to

the Contessa during one of the long and frequent absences of the Count. She was a splendid young creature, of twenty-two, but looking at least five-and-twenty. Her dark complexion had a translucency about it that gave it a singular eloquence and charm. Her cheeks were rich in the carnation of youth and health. Her eyes were those of the gazelle; and above her rather low brow the thick ripples of blue-black hair waved in beautiful luxuriance, and were gathered together in two thick, long, Clothilde plaits tied with red ribbon, and which reached down to the middle of her fine, tapering leg. This densely black hair matched the ebon arch of her eyebrows and the long lashes that hung from the upper and under lids of her glorious eyes. Her nose was delicately aquiline, her upper lip short and curved, her well-chiselled lips were of the richest vermilion, and her teeth were like two rows of Roman pearls.

She was a young Diana in form, with the broad shoulders, full bust, short waist, column-like throat, and powerful, well-shaped limbs that mark the child of the people. She wore the half-military, half-peasant costume of her country, in which a good deal of black velvet, gold braid, white muslin, and scarlet, set off her singular and most picturesque beauty. The Contessa took a fancy to Jocunda at once. The strong, healthy, young Sicilian, who had never known a care, whose cheek was, indeed, "unprofaned by a tear," felt her good, kind heart soften and warm towards the fair, delicate, and unhappy-looking being, who, in years a girl like herself, had that drooping, care-worn air, those pale cheeks and swollen eye-lids, that air of self-neglect and self-abandonment, and that scared, crushed, forlorn look, which, in all lands, and all times, bespeaks the unloved, unhappy, down-trodden, and frightened wife.

The young love the young; and, in spite of all old Perpetua's rules, lectures, threats, and promises (for Perpetua had no sympathy with the "pale, sickly mope," as she called Georgina), all the young Jocunda's energies were secretly directed to cheering and comforting the young Contessa, and preparing for the little stranger, of whom she spoke with a love and enthusiasm generally only bestowed on the little one already born into this world of sin and sorrow. Not that, to Jocunda, it was the world of sin and sorrow which it had proved to her young mistress. Jocunda was as innocent as the wild-flowers she loved to gather, and as glad and merry as the birds in the air, and the kids that leaped from crag to crag. But she was full of daring, courage, moral and physical strength. She knew no fear; and, though all the young fellows in the neighbourhood were in love with Jocunda, she, as yet, knew the master-passion only by name; for, though her heart was not a little inclined to favour Renzo—a brave and bold young fisherman, who would have died to serve her—she, as yet, felt only for him that growing preference, and that dawning interest, which may or may not ripen into love.

The doubt kept the handsome young Renzo in a fever of suspense, an agony of devotion, and a perfect thraldom of attentions and homage. He was very glad when he heard that Jocunda was going to reside at the Castle, because his little fishing hut was situated among the rocks about ten minutes' walk from the spot; and when he put out to sea in the morning he could see her waving her graceful hand to him, and at night a light in her window told him that if she would not own him as her acknowledged lover, he was still in her thoughts, and that perhaps that light was meant as a beacon to guard, and a star to light him on to an Eden of love and joy.

CHAPTER XVII.

"No radiant pearl that crested Fortune wears,
No gem that twinkling hangs from Beauty's ears,
Nor the bright stars that heaven's blue arch adorn,
Nor rubies bright that deck the early morn,
Shine with such radiance as the tear that breaks,
For other's woe, down Woman's lovely cheeks!"

ANON.

THE Contessa and Jocunda soon understood each other. The former quickly learnt the soft Sicilian dialect that flowed like music from the scarlet lips of her maid; and Jocunda began to speak the prettiest broken English, picking it up as it fell from the pale lips of the unhappy Contessa.

The Count and his free companions had

been some weeks absent, but several of the rough, wild, serving-men remained behind to guard the castle, assist old Perpetua in all her household labours, even in those of a house-maid and cook, and by their fishing, shooting, and gardening, to supply the table. These dark, moustachioed, bearded fellows were all armed; and the Contessa, accustomed to the well-trained servants of the Hauteville establishment (one of the most perfectly appointed in England), smiled a faint smile when she saw these bandits scrubbing the floors, dusting, washing, preparing the vegetables, and watching the roast or boiled, all kept in strict order, in spite of their daggers and pistols, by the shrill tongue and termagant temper of old Perpetua.

By degrees, as the Contessa and Jocunda began to understand each other better, the former poured out her filial penitence, her wedded misery, and her growing fears, into the sympathizing, devoted bosom of the zealous Jocunda. The young Sicilian had great natural shrewdness, perception, and tact. These qualities in her supplied the place of experience and knowledge of the world. She knew nothing of reversions and life-assurances, but when the Contessa explained to her what had been done, Jocunda shook her raven tresses, and, as delicately and cautiously as she could, she informed her mistress that the Count had a dreadful name—that Jacopo, his head man, was a remorseless villain—that terrible crimes were laid to the charge of both, and she advised her to dissimulate—to appear to suspect nothing—but, as soon as her child was born, and her health required to be restored, to make an excuse to go to the baths of L—— for a little change, and thence to make her escape to England, never to return.

"Oh! Jocunda, I dare not. I have no

courage—no energy. If I failed, he would recapture and kill me."

"But you should not fail, sweet lady," said Jocunda. "I will go with you—I will help you; and Renzo, of whom I spoke to you, Eccellenza" (and here a slight blush mantled her animated face), "he shall help us. By the Holy Virgin, he shall enable you to escape, or he may give me up, and hang himself, or marry humpbacked Bertha."

"But we can do nothing yet, Jocunda," said the Contessa, with the timid, procrastinating spirit of the cowed, down-trodden wife. "It is not necessary yet. I must stay here till after my confinement; I could not escape now."

"I know not that, dear lady," said Jocunda. "It were better your child were born among those flinty rocks than in this castle. But you look pale, Eccellenza, I will say no more at present, we will talk of this when you feel better. I overheard Beppo tell my grandmother that the Count will not be back for six weeks, at which time he expects to be a father."

"Oh! thank Heaven! he is not coming for six weeks, then!" said the Contessa, clasping her thin, white hands.

"They were so wan and transparent of hue,
You might have seen the moon shine through."

"Oh! Jocunda, what a relief is that! Every morning and every evening I pray that God in his mercy may take me and my expected babe to himself before the Count returns to curse me, as he did ere he departed."

And this was the young girl of some ten months back, who had so cunningly deceived her parents, so adroitly wrought her own ruin, and realized the romance of a foreign alliance and a love-match.

CHAPTER XVIII.

"Unhappy woman! still thy lot shall be
A dream of love, or a reality
Of unshared sorrow; raise your heart, you need
A firmer pillar than the broken reed
Of man's affection! Why will you bestow
On *him* the worship which to God you owe?
Know you the cause of all your careworn years,
Your days of watching, and your nights of tears?
Love you, and are you sad? and would you know
Why tale of Love is ever traced in woe?
Ask—ask your heart: you've reared an idol there;
You've laid up treasures, with mistaken zeal,
Where moth and rust corrupt, where thieves break
through and steal!"

BRIDE OF SIENA.

ONE bright but windy night, just before the Contessa undressed, preparatory to seeking her couch (Jocunda and herself had been working till a late hour for the expected one), loud screams in the entrance-hall below caught the ear of both. Jocunda started to her feet, and ran upstairs to rouse Perpetua, and to get a dagger which the old crone kept under her pillow. She begged the Contessa to await her return; and Georgina would certainly not have ventured down alone, but that the shrieks which had disturbed her were mingled with English ejaculations, in a voice familiar to her ear! Yes, it was the well-known voice the poor Contessa had so often longed to hear again—the voice of the constant companion of her girlhood—her sister Augusta!

Without a thought of self, the Contessa rushed down stairs, and there, by the light of the hall-lamp, she saw two of her husband's free companions—the one was carrying a lady who had fainted, the other was struggling with a fair, dishevelled young creature, who shrieked wildly, and resisted all his efforts to drag her along. Despair gave her strength, and she clung to the door-sill. The door was open, and the sea, flooded by the silver radiance of the moon, was to be seen in all the glory of both.

"Beppo," cried the Contessa in Italian, "let the lady go—she is my sister! Augusta," she cried, "do you not see me?—do you not know me?—do you not recognise your unhappy Georgina?"

In a moment the sisters were in each other's arms; and Beppo and Marco, all ruffians as they were, felt there was something sacred in that meeting—something holy in those tears, and presumed not to interfere. The Contessa then led the way to her own apartments, and Jocunda was soon at hand to help her to comfort and assist Lady Richlands and her companion, an Italian of great beauty. Lady Richlands (the reader will remember that Augusta Hauteville had accepted her sister's forsaken old Earl) gave the following account of her being thus violently brought to the Castello.

She said that the Earl of Richlands had latterly taken great delight in yachting; that at Naples he had formed an intimacy with some Italian noblemen, who had advised him to visit Sicily; that the Earl, herself, and a Neapolitan lady introduced by one of these Italians, had set sail for Sicily, and that within a mile of the castle they had been attacked by pirates, boarded, conquered, and carried off by force. What had become of the Earl, and of the money and valuables she had on board the yacht, Lady Richlands did not know. But she was so enchanted to find herself under her sister's roof, that she did not seem disposed to give way to despair at the possibility that the old Earl might have been taken captive.

Beppo, resolving to keep strict watch over the doors, was obliged to allow the Contessa's sister to share her apartment.

The beautiful Neapolitan had a room assigned her, and the Contessa was much disposed to treat her with great confidence, as a sharer of her sister's misfortunes, and of her "moving accidents by flood and field."

However, a hint from Jocunda put her on her guard. When the Neapolitan was safe in her own room, Jocunda closed the Contessa's doors, and said, in a whisper:

"Eccellenza, beware of the Neapolitan; she is no stranger here. Even I distinctly remember her features in the long ago, and I am certain some deep plot brings her here now! She was not in the swoon she shammed so well; for I remarked, as Beppo carried her upstairs, she took care to move so as to avoid being hurt by the banisters and the door-posts. I think my grandmother knows all about her, but she is as close as wax. I saw looks of intelligence exchanged between her and the men; I am certain she is here for no good!

I believe she is a woman who occasionally lives here with the Count, and I know it was said that she was a slow and secret poisoner: she has an evil eye. Dear ladies, I much fear there is no time to be lost! If the Count returns, we are powerless. What say you?—have you strength, have you courage, to escape to-night?"

"Oh, but those terrible men!" said the Contessa, shivering, and growing pale as the Dead.

"I have left the brandy on the table, as if by accident," said Jocunda; "they will drink deep, and sleep soundly. I have instructed Renzo to be in readiness; and I have told him, if, when he looks up at my window, before going to bed, he sees two lights instead of one, he is to row at once, in his fishing-boat, under these windows, by the terrace steps outside. We can easily get into the boat without disturbing those ruffians. I feel certain it is your only chance, Eccellenza; do not throw it away! That woman's arrival bodes you no good! Let me put up a few things in a basket, and take, dear lady, all your valuables. Renzo can row you to a place of safety. I feel as if Providence dictated my words!"

Still the Contessa shrank and hesitated, but her sister and Jocunda decided for her.

Jocunda signalled to her lover, and ere long the light splash of his oars was heard beneath the windows; and his boat, black and broad, and very safe, rose and fell with the undulation of the silver waves.

Jocunda had put up all the baby-linen prepared for the little stranger, the Contessa's jewels, and what little money she had, and a few changes and comforts. She had ventured down to the foot of the stairs to listen, and had ascertained that the men were in the dead sleep of inebriety.

The Contessa was almost helpless with fear; but, with the aid of Jocunda and her sister (Lady Richlands), she was wrapped up in a large, black, hooded cloak, and placed in the boat. Lightly Lady Richlands and Jocunda sprang in after her; and Renzo, plying his oars as if for his own life and liberty, sent the boat swiftly along. The cool night breeze nerved the Contessa, who

> "Felt her brow become more light
> Beneath the freshness of the night;"

and, to enliven the ladies (when they were out of earshot), Jocunda and Renzo chanted the Sicilian Mariners' hymn, in the rich, deep voices of the south; and the melody, the moonlight, the sense of her sister's presence, and of Jocunda's fidelity and devotion, filled the Contessa's heart with hope and comfort; her head drooped on Jocunda's broad shoulders, and, ere long, a soft, sweet sleep closed her weary eyelids—the first refreshing sleep she had known for many a long month!

Renzo knew of a safe shelter among the rocks. It was a place where he had often moored his boat, and it possessed a cave, in which he advised that the ladies should remain hidden during the glare of day; and that when night again set in, he should row them on, until they met with some vessel which could convey them to a port whence they could embark for England.

It was bright moonlight when they entered the cave. Renzo moored his boat behind a jutting angle of rock, where it could not be seen from the castle side of the coast; and then he busied himself in helping Jocunda to make things comfortable for the Contessa and her sister.

Jocunda had brought a good supply of cushions, shawls, and a rug, and as there was clean, dry straw in the corner of the cave, Renzo and Jocunda soon contrived, with the shawls and the rug to make a comfortable couch whereon the ladies could repose. She had forgotten nothing; and Renzo, by her commands, began to kindle a fire among the rocks outside, to fetch water from a rill that trickled in a silvery stream down the rocks, and to boil the same.

Soon the fragrant steam of coffee saluted the nostrils of the recumbent, half-sleeping sisters. Renzo was in the seventh heaven. It was such ecstasy to him to be permitted to help Jocunda, to be by her side, to be praised, consulted, or even scolded by her, to feel her sweet breath wave his thick clustering black hair, and fan his bronzed, manly cheek, now and then to touch her hand, or even the hem of her garment—all this was ecstasy. "Trifles make the sum of human things," and this beautiful truth applies especially to the inner life of love. A kind glance can ensure happy days and nights of sweet repose. A cold look, a frown, or a haughty, sarcastic smile have, ere this, driven Passion to Suicide. Oh! then, ye who are loved, beware how you trifle with the great and sacred power bestowed upon you!—

> "The rose we wear upon the heart,
> Should have no thorn to wound us."

Jocunda, we must own it, *was* a little overbearing, exacting, and tyrannical, but Renzo was a very good-humoured young fellow, and he could see that there was a growing softness in Jocunda's black eyes, even while she scolded him with her soft Sicilian tongue, or even when she hit him (hard, though in sport) an occasional slap with her large, well-shaped hand.

Jocunda had forgotten nothing—coffee, cream, sugar, cakes. The Contessa had a small English travelling-case, with tea and coffee pot, two cups, &c., &c. This Jocunda had brought with her, and, after the ladies had done, Renzo and his beloved repaired to an outer cavern in the rock, out of hearing, that they might not disturb the Contessa and her sister, and there they, too, feasted on the coffee and the cakes, and Renzo on the love that was filling his own heart to an overflow, and on that which he began to fancy trembled in Jocunda's voice, fluttered at her full bosom, beamed in her eyes, and translated itself into blushes on her cheeks, and into smiles on her lips.

The Contessa and Lady Richlands slept the deep, dreamless sleep of intense fatigue. Locked as they were in those slumbers, the young Renzo and Jocunda were alone. That "sun of the sleepless" (the moon) was shining on the ocean, and looking into the maid's pure, deep Sicilian eyes, and Renzo led her by the hand out of the cave to roam by the glorious sea. He adored her, passionately adored her; and she was alone with the moon and him!—but yet she was safe. There is a sort of reverence in true love. No thought she would have blushed to hear or to inspire darkened the heart where her fair image was enshrined. Protected by her own innocence and by his honour, they roamed on, on, on, hand in hand—bright, beautiful, beloved. Hero and her Leander might have looked thus, in the light of the moon that silvered the Hellespont.

Suddenly Renzo drew Jocunda behind a projecting rock, whispering to her,

"Hush! stoop down, keep closer, they come!"

"Who come?" said Jocunda, in a frightened whisper.

"The Count, Beppo, Jacopo, and several others."

"They have, then, discovered our escape, and they are in pursuit! Doubtless they think we have fled on foot and are gone to

——. They have not dreamt of the boat and of you, Renzo."

"No matter, if you have, *carissima,*" said Renzo, kissing her hand, and receiving a box on the ear in return.

"How can you sport at such a time?" said the maid.

"Why, we are safe; we may well sport. The Contessa is saved. They will go on to B——."

As he spoke, several horsemen galloped past the rocks where our lovers were hidden. Their horses' hoofs seemed to fly across the hard, smooth, silvery sands. It was low water; and Renzo, cautiously peering from behind the angle of crag, exclaimed,

"*Per Bacco!* there is a woman of the party! Who and what may she be? A fine figure, too! She rides well, and her long hair floats in the moonbeams like a black banner. Who is she?"

"Hast thou never heard of a Neapolitan, who was here some three years ago? They called her Petronella, the slow poisoner."

"Oh!" said Renzo, with a shudder, "I do remember her. The old Count and Contessa died during her stay here."

"Ay, Renzo; and but for thee and thy brave help, this night the young Contessa would have shared their fate."

"Thou art pleased with thy poor Renzo?" And he stole his strong arm round her waist.

"Very," she faltered; and her head sank on his shoulder.

"And may I claim a reward?"

"Yes; but only to be granted when she, poor lady, is safe."

"So be it," said Renzo. "And, in the meantime, seal that promise with one kiss —oh, my Jocunda!"

Jocunda knew not how it happened; she

was certain, in thinking of it afterwards, that she never consented. She was, in all such matters, not merely a prude, but a very pugnacious prude; and long as Renzo had loved, nay, idolised her, he had never even kissed her hand before that happy night. But yet it was a fact that he did, she knew not how, steal Love's first kiss from her sweet virgin lips—"a long, long kiss, a kiss of youth and love;" and that on her scolding and complaining of what she blushingly called a theft, he, wild with joy, exclaiming he would set all right by putting the kiss back again on the very spot whence he stole it, repeated the offence, and was a long time in getting Jocunda to forgive him; and this she would only do upon his promising never to attempt the like again, until good old Father Filippo had joined their hands in the little church of Santa Maria, among the hills, where both had been wont from infancy to pray, and where both had made their first communion, and where both were wont to confess their little peccadilloes, in default of great sins. To ensure obedience, and not to lead herself or her betrothed into temptation, Jocunda, ordering him to try and compose himself to sleep in the outer cave, stole into that where the Contessa and her sister, Lady Richlands, slept; and just as the sun came forth in triumph, to tread the path which Aurora had strewn with fresh roses, Renzo in the outer and Jocunda in the inner cave, passed through the crystal gates of sleep into the blissful Dreamland.

* * * * *

All through that bright and sunny day our wearied wanderers slept. The soft ripple of the waves and the wild hum of the bee, as he passed from one bright rock-cactus to another, were their lullaby.

At night they awoke, rested and refreshed;

and Renzo, by the light of the moon, rowed them on, on, on, until a yacht—an English yacht—appeared, silvered by that moon, at a little distance, and English voices gladdened their ears. To their "Boat, ahoy!" Renzo answered by shouting out, in Italian, that two English ladies in distress begged to be taken aboard.

The *Nautilus*, upon this, soon shot to their rescue. Lord Claremont, the kind, jolly, and noble captain of the *Nautilus*, was an old friend of Lady Richlands, and had picked up the old earl, her husband, who, when the supposed pirates boarded the steamer she was in, and carried off herself and the Signora Petronella, had been left to sink or swim as fate might decree.

The poor old Earl, who had lost his wig, his porcelain teeth, and his dressing-case in the conflict, and whose rouge and false eyebrows had been washed off by the rude waves, was ensconsed for concealment in a berth, and thus the Contessa escaped an interview with her forsaken adorer.

The question now arose, what was to become of Jocunda? The Contessa, Lady Richlands, and all the gentlemen (Lord Claremont at their head) tried to persuade Jocunda, whom they ardently admired, to embark on board the *Nautilus.*

Renzo was silent, but there were volumes of love and entreaty in his dark, appealing eyes; and, more irresistible still, there was a tear glittering on the black lashes, and a deadly pallor on the bronzed cheek; and they prevailed.

"No, Eccellenza—no, kind lords," she said; "I promised Renzo to be his wife when I had seen that the Contessa was safe. The Contessa is safe now. He will row me back to the shore; we shall repair at once to the church of Santa Maria, among the hills; and there the good old Father Filippo will join our hands. Farewell, dear lady! Addio, addio, addio!"

Renzo, at these words, threw his arm round his bride elect, and waved his red fisherman's cap in token of triumph and adieu, while she bowed her graceful head, and the noble captain and the crew on board the *Nautilus* cheered lustily; and then the splendid English yacht and the broad-bottomed, black old Sicilian fishing-boat parted company. The former was bound for Naples in the first instance, and Dover in the next; the latter for the nearest point to the little church of Santa Maria among the wild hills. Both reached in safety the havens where they would be.

The good old Father Filippo gladly joined the hands of the young pair, whom he had baptized, and in whose innocent confessions each other's names had so often figured.

Renzo led Jocunda, bathed in blushes, from

that altar to the little fisherman's cot, which she was to convert into an Eden of the heart.

> "Happy, happy, happy pair!
> None but the brave,
> None but the brave,
> None but the brave deserve the fair."

And Renzo *was* brave—Renzo had deserved the fair. He had won that pearl of price, a maiden's heart; he won it well, and may he wear it long!

CHAPTER XIX.

> "No matter what the age, the form, the face,
> There is in virtue such resistless grace;
> The old, the ugly, may the fair control,
> If he reveal nobility of soul."
>
> LASCELLES.

THERE *was* something fine about the old Earl of Richlands. There generally is something great, beneath the bubbles of vanity and folly, in the heart of an English nobleman. Froth and straws may float on the surface, and cold waters, that chill and repel, may shock away sympathy; but there are gems of value in the caves beneath.

And so with the vain, made-up old Earl. He would not let his young wife see him in his dilapidated state, denuded of all his artificial charms. He was resolved she should not have one glimpse of his person until his valet, and the artists in teeth, hair, and complexion, had restored him to his former self. But for the first time he let his young wife see into his heart—his inner self; and this glimpse of his true nature did more to win her love and fealty, than all that Art had effected in patching up his face and form.

The Contessa, remembering how she had jilted him, feared he would refuse to allow his young wife to receive and to shelter her. Augusta, Countess of Richlands, herself felt very uneasy on the subject. Both sisters were very much relieved, and the wife was touched to the heart, when a note, written by the Earl in pencil (from his berth), was put into Lady Richlands' hands. He simply said:—

"I am sorry, my darling Augusta, that I cannot at present receive you and your fair sister, and congratulate you both on the miraculous escape, of which I do not at present know the full particulars; but my nervous system has been so much impaired by this shipwreck, I have caught so severe a cold, and am so much disfigured in my personal appearance, that I cannot bear to present myself before you until I am in some degree recovered and restored. To your lovely sister, my Augusta, present my brotherly regards and warmest sympathy. Tell her that her sister's husband will be in all respects a brother to her; that our sympathy shall comfort, our love cherish her, our roof shelter, and our protection shield her. Beg her, my darling Augusta, to rest assured that no harm I can avert shall ever befall one who is the sister of the idolised wife of

"RICHLANDS."

Oh! if men who really covet the love of their wives, and are jealous of their tenderness, did but know how their hearts respond to any act of generosity to those dear to them from the cradle, they would surely take as much pains to make their relatives welcome and happy in their homes, as they often do to estrange and annoy them.

For the *first* time (as she read this kind and generous letter) Augusta's heart *warmed* towards the Earl, and she inwardly vowed to be a good, a true, a loving, and a faithful wife to one who had proved that he had such true nobility of soul, such a sublime power of forgiveness of what a vain man hardly ever does forgive—the being jilted, on the eve of marriage, with a girl young enough to be his daughter.

It is wonderful how much good a man does himself with his wife, by proving himself in any degree worthy of the homage he is so ready to exact, and which she so gladly pays, when she can persuade herself it is deserved.

"Your home will henceforth be with us, Georgina," said the young Countess of Richlands, fondly embracing the pale Contessa, whom her former lover's generosity had convulsed with sobs and tears. "You will not be obliged to face mamma."

"No! no! no! I could never have done that. I could work, beg, starve; but I could never go home to my parents. I could never endure mamma's reproaches, papa's cold and silent scorn. How shall I prove my gratitude to him I so heartlessly——"

"Oh! don't trouble your head about that," said Augusta, colouring; "leave that to me. *I* can reward him, and I will, never fear."

Augusta was beginning to feel even a little jealous of the Earl's former preference for her sister. She is proud of him now! Well done, old Earl of Richlands! wert thou ten times more made up in face and form than thou art, the evidence thou hast just given of a generous nature, a great soul, and a noble mind, would win the love of any true woman's heart!

CHAPTER XX.

> "How much a fool that has been sent to Rome
> Excels a fool that has been kept at home!"
>
> COWPER.

Two years have passed pleasantly away on the Continent with Mrs. Croft and her travelling party. Arthur, to the surprise of every one who looked upon him as the poor, dependent, adopted grandson of Lawyer Croft, has been entered at Oxford, after five years as an oppidan at Eton. His vacations are spent on the Continent, as are those of young Croft, Lord Pontecraft, and the eldest son of the house of Hauteville. The old Earl of Rockalpine still lives— a life devoted to piety and good deeds. He corresponds regularly with his darling, Edith Lorraine; he still attends to her poor at Rockalpine, and enables her to do much in judicious charity abroad.

Young Croft is become madly enamoured of Edith, and the passion of his crony, Lord Pontecraft, keeps pace with his. But Arthur is still what he has been from her childhood—the one idol of her fancy, the one darling of her heart.

From a sickly but sweet-looking girl, Edith is grown into the loveliest, most delicately blooming, and most fascinating of young women. The once red hair is now of the richest and most golden brown; and the figure which Lady Hauteville and her doctors had doomed to perpetual deformity, is now a shape that,

> "Given to marble, had immortalised a name."

And all this time Lady Hauteville, who so values, or rather overvalues, the "power of grace" and "Beauty's heavenly ray," thinks and talks of our lovely heroine as "poor little Edith, the carroty cripple," doomed to perpetual spinsterhood.

Her third daughter, Ida, is now in her second season, and as yet has had no offer. She has been much admired (especially at her *début*), but she sees her chances diminish every week. The old millionaire, Sir J. Brownlow, has shown some symptoms of liking; but Ida scorned them in her first season, and now she would not refuse even him.

Lady Hauteville does not see much of her daughter, the Countess of Richlands, because she is so bitter against the unfortunate Contessa, whom she will not forgive, and the Earl of Richlands is so devoted a champion of his poor sister-in-law. The Earl's charms are all restored, and his cheek is more pink, his eyebrows more jetty in their perfect arch, his teeth more glittering, and his Hyperion curls more glossy and more fragrant than ever.

He is padded into perfect symmetry, and the *old* man is only to be detected in the stiffness of his gait. He is the very proudest and happiest of men, for his Countess has presented him with an heir. He has redeemed his pledge, and is indeed a brother to the poor Contessa, who has never heard one word of her ruffian husband since her miraculous escape.

The poor Contessa was not destined to be a happy mother. How could a treacherous and undutiful daughter expect the great, all-atoning blessing of maternity? Her terrors and griefs ended in the birth of a still-born child (a daughter). She narrowly escaped with her own blighted life.

Mrs. Croft, who has found money fly as fast, if not faster, on the Continent than in England, has taken a villa, for a year, in the neighbourhood of Zurich. And hither, at Christmas, Arthur had come to spend his vacation with them. He was to be followed, soon after, by Roger Croft, Lord Pontecraft, and Edith's brother, Marcus Lorraine.

The villa was at about six miles' distance from Zurich, and Arthur had, hitherto, always walked from Zurich, leaving his luggage to come in a cart. Hitherto, also, Edith, attended by a servant, had contrived to meet him in a forest about a mile from the villa.

When she rose on the morning of the day upon which Arthur was expected, she saw that a heavy fall of snow covered the landscape. She said nothing, fearing that Mrs Croft might insist on her not venturing out; but, full of love, impatience, and the fear of disappointing Arthur, she seized her opportunity when Mrs. Croft was rating all her servants in the kitchen, and, putting on her goloshes and her hooded plaid cloak, she sallied forth alone.

The paths of the villa garden had been swept, the road to the little hamlet was trodden down; and it was not till Edith got out into the open country that she began to fear that she should never find the road through the forest. Everything looked so different; the country, of which she knew every path, was now all strange to her! To add to her despair, a fierce north wind set in, and chilled her young blood; down, too, in blinding, bewildering drifts came the snow!

On, on, on, for a full hour plodded poor Edith, and then the sudden conviction forced itself upon her mind that she had lost her way; that Arthur would think she had not cared to meet him; that the cold was numbing her limbs, and rendering further progress impossible; that she was weary, dreary, desolate, half-dead with exhaustion and fatigue, and very likely to be frozen to death. As this dreadful conviction forced itself upon her mind, her strength and endurance gave way at once, and she sank down at the outskirts of that forest through which her pathway lay.

There, some hours later, on their way home from work with their yoked bullocks, two woodcutters found her, as they thought, frozen to death.

"She belongs to the Villa Bellevue," said one. "She is that pretty young English girl who always smiles so kindly when we meet her in the forest."

"And gave us something to drink her health the other day," replied the other. "Lend a hand; let's wrap her up, place her on the charrette, and take her to the villa. She's numbed and asleep, but I don't believe she's dead."

Very tenderly the Swiss woodcutters raised the half-frozen girl, and placing her on their rustic truck, hurried away with her to the villa.

* * * * *

There was great consternation and terror at

Bellevue Villa when it was discovered that Edith Lorraine was missing.

Arthur, who had reckoned on meeting her at least in the avenue of fir-trees at the entrance of the villa, felt hurt, slighted, and disappointed when he found she was not there.

First love is so sensitive, so exacting, so susceptible to the smallest change, neglect, or slight! But its moods are as fitful as those of an April day; and after the first heart-crushing emotions of disappointment and wounded feeling, came a reaction in the thought that, perhaps, Edith was ill! It was so unlike *her* to disappoint the heart that secretly adored her! Edith—generous, devoted, delicate Edith—she always delighted to surpass her lover's expectations! If he gave her the strong, passionate, exclusive love of his young, ardent heart, sweet Edith repaid him measure for measure. There was not one jot of coquetry, one shade of artifice, one iota of vanity in the nature of Edith Lorraine.

The Misses Croft were full of worldly maxims, instilled by their mamma, such as, "Fly, and they'll follow; follow, and they'll fly;" "By keeping them off, you'll keep them on;" and, "You'll never be dear if you make yourself cheap." Even Gloriana had learnt to toss her head, and arch her neck, and affect indifference; but Edith was all truth, tenderness, devotion. She loved Arthur as Virginia loved Paul, and Arthur loved her as Paul loved Virginia.

Of course, Mrs. Croft could not be quite blind to the strong affection that bound these fair and noble young creatures together. But she affected to treat it as a childish friendship—a brother and sister love! She knew that the old Earl of Rockalpine had left to his darling Edith everything that was not strictly entailed on his heir, Lord Hauteville. Mrs. Croft was not above occasionally lingering at doors or peeping into letters! She knew that, as it was owing to Edith and her holy influence that the old man had been induced to lay up treasures in Heaven, he had left the hoards of a life to her.

She knew, then, that Edith, at the Earl's death, would not only be Lady Edith Lorraine, but heiress to fabulous wealth; she knew that her son—her Roger, in her partial eyes the most modish, handsome, and fascinating of young men—loved sweet Edith, with such love as such natures can feel; that a passionate desire to possess and be master of a creature so lovely and loveable was wisely blent, in her Roger, with the ambition to ally himself with the great house of Rockalpine; to have (as he said) a handle to his wife's name, even if he could have none to his own: and to secure the heiress of the old Earl's wealth before he died, and before it was known to the world and to Lady Hauteville, that poor little Edith, "the carroty cripple," to whom she had destined two hundred a year, to live as a deformed spinster at Croft Villa, was an auburn Aphroditè in face and form, and heiress to all the hoards of her miser grandfather.

There were great difficulties in the way of getting her fast, over-dressed, under-bred, cigar-smoking, casino and Cremorne frequenting Roger united to the delicate and heart-stirring Edith; but both mother and son so highly estimated the attractions of Mr. Croft, junior, that they agreed that it *was* "on the cards."

One great impediment arose (as they fancied) not in the form of Arthur, whom they both secretly hated and despised, but in that of Roger's Eton and Oxford chum, Lord Pontecraft. He loved Edith; and, as heir to the Marquis of Dunstanburgh and his immense estates and boundless wealth, he felt he had only to ask and have—to propose and be accepted. He had no Belgravian mamma to plot and counterplot—no sisters to pick out flaws in sweet Edith, and to try to entangle him with some dear Lady Laura or Lady Harriette, whose brother they were aiming at for themselves. The old Marquis, his father, was a martyr to gout, and could not live long; and once a Marquis himself, he would propose to Lord and Lady Hauteville (whom, as yet, he only knew by name) for their enchanting Edith; and he did not imagine he should meet with a refusal from them.

He was a cold-mannered, hot-headed, warm-hearted aristocrat, with an overweening notion of his own importance; tall, well-made, with a pale, Grecian face, inherited from his mother, a fine forehead, a well-curved lip, and a heart that had never failed to throb to a generous sentiment, or been conscious of the power of love, except in its secret and wilful passion for Edith Lorraine.

Roger Croft was the toady of this young aristocrat. Roger Croft flattered him, imitated him, swore by him. Lord Pontecraft quizzed Roger Croft, made use of him, and swore at him. In his heart Roger hated the young Lord, and anticipated with inward exultation the delight of outwitting him, and of marrying the only object whose presence had ever sent a flush to Lord Pontecraft's marble cheek, a ray to his cold blue eye, or a throb to his strange proud heart. But, while resolved to marry Edith himself, Roger was the confidant of his noble friend's passion, and pretended to encourage, to approve, and to be ready to assist.

Roger treated Arthur with a ludicrous degree of coldness and *hauteur*, and had tried all he could to embitter his Eton career. Roger Croft, and a good many "nobs" of his set, had contrived, by hints, inuendoes, and vile anonymous letters, to convey to the boys, and even the masters, that Arthur was an illegitimate, penniless lad, adopted by his father out of caprice.

Birth and wealth are a good deal esteemed at Eton by masters and pupils, but scholarship and "pluck" have greater influence still. Arthur, with the idea fully impressed upon his mind that he had nothing but his scholarship to depend upon, worked very hard, and was soon far above Roger Croft and Lord Pontecraft.

Then, too, he was both very brave and very good-humoured. At cricket and at rowing he was pre-eminent, so that soon he had a strong party in the school.

Roger Croft was a great bully; and Arthur, having traced a vile slander to him, challenged him (big as he was, and four years Arthur's senior), fought him, and thrashed him soundly.

"Croft's set" grew much more cautious and civil after this. They took warning from the fact that Roger Croft had two black eyes, and two front teeth broken.

That fracture neither Roger Croft nor his mother ever forgave. Yet it was his own fault, for the meanness of his underhand endeavour to injure poor Arthur deserved a more severe punishment. But as his front teeth projected, and were very large, he was immensely disfigured by the breaking of them, and spoke with a thick lisp ever after.

At Oxford, Roger Croft and his "fast set" both tried to injure Arthur in the opinion of the men they thought most of; but many of his Eton chums remained his fast friends at Oxford.

And now we must accompany Arthur from *Alma Mater* to the Villa Bellevue, and describe the agony of his alarm when it became certain that Edith was nowhere to be found. He was rushing frantically about the country, unconscious of the bitter cold and fast-falling snow, when he suddenly encountered the woodcutters, and on their *charrette* beheld the slight form of Edith.

The men motioned to him not to arouse her; and Arthur, in an agony of suspense, walked by the side of the *charrette;* and when it stopped at the doors of the villa, he caught the apparently lifeless form of the young girl in his arms, and carried her up into what he knew was her own room.

Mrs. Croft, her daughters, and the maids of the household soon rushed in. One of them, an old cook, was fortunately a sensible woman, and well acquainted with the means to be used to restore animation in cases of drowning, freezing, &c. Luckily, the room, which was heated—as all rooms in Zurich are—by a large earthenware stove, was well-warmed; and a bright wood fire blazed in an open fire-place (a great rarity in that country) in Edith's dressing-room. Friction, stimulants, a warm bath, and a warm bed were tried; and Arthur, necessarily driven away, was pacing the landing outside Edith's door, and praying fervently. Presently the old cook, who felt for his suspense and anxiety, went out to tell him that animation was restored; that warmth had returned to the body, colour to the lips and cheeks; that the pulse could be felt, and the breathing heard; and that the young lady had sunk into a soft, deep sleep.

Upon this, Arthur implored so passionately to be allowed to see her for a moment, that the kind old cook (*pro tempore* nurse) could not refuse to permit him (under many restrictions) to approach Edith's bedside.

CHAPTER XXI.

"—— None such joy are reaping
As those who watch o'er what they love while sleeping."
BYRON.

POOR Arthur! when he entered the darkened chamber (generally so full of life and light, but in which at that moment a shaded lamp threw a sickly gleam on every object), and saw the idol of his heart lying in a death-like sleep, white and cold as marble, her rich long auburn hair, damp with the snow, scattered over the pillow, and lilac tints round her closed eyes and sweet mouth, he sank on his knees beside the bed in an agony of grief and fear. He hid his face in the snowy quilt of the young girl's bed, and, in spite of all his manhood, all his self-control, hot tears gushed from his eyes, and choking sobs contracted his throat and convulsed his breast.

Two of the Croft girls were watching the lovely patient, while the cook-nurse, Lisbeth, went to her supper. Gloriana, grown into a pretty young woman, was standing in real anxiety and sorrow at the foot of the bed, almost tearing her pocket-handkerchief, as busy Memory would recall to awakened Conscience many little unkindnesses (prompted by spite, envy, and jealousy) which she had done to poor Edith; many angry, cross, and bitter words, many petty slanders and wilful misconstructions, and all in return for goodness that was never weary either in word or deed, soft answers that turn away any wrath but that of Envy, and countless services great and small—all felt, acknowledged, and remembered, perhaps too late!

The eldest Miss Croft, quite as blameable,

but much more hardened, was smiling, a little bitterly, perhaps, at Arthur's anguish. Arthur, generally so collected, so reticent, so dignified with these, his half-aunts and whole enemies, to be seen so prostrated by grief and terror as to sob and weep! But a malicious, heartless woman must that be, who could look on such a scene with a sneer, or who could ever see a man weep, or could hear a man sob, without melting into tears herself.

* * * * * *

The doctor was not very sanguine about Edith's recovery. The exhaustion was so great, and there was so little re-action, for Edith had never been strong or robust. Everything, Dr. Richter (he was a Swiss) said, would depend on the most careful nursing; that all through the night Edith must have some restorative administered every quarter of an hour—chicken-jelly, strong broth, brandy—these must be given in very small quantities, but at regular intervals. The fire must be kept up, so that the room should be constantly at a certain temperature, and hot bottles must be kept to the feet.

Arthur heard all this, and noted every word. His own life was bound up in Edith's, and he resolved to watch. The Misses Croft, Gloriana, especially, begged to be permitted to sit up with Edith, but "mamma," who was very anxious about their looks, particularly as Roger Croft was expected to bring some young men of family and fortune over with him on a visit to Bellevue Villa, would not hear of it. As for herself, she declared she was quite unfit to nurse Edith for an hour, so terrible had been the shock which her nervous system had sustained, by the absence and alarming condition of the dear girl whom she had reared and cherished as her own. No, Lisbeth was willing to take charge of Edith Lorraine—Lisbeth, the cook, at one time a regular nurse, accustomed to sit up at night, and every way suited for the responsibility.

Arthur said nothing, but he inwardly vowed that, if Lisbeth watched Edith, he would take care to watch Lisbeth. Lisbeth, a good, hard-working creature, who rose every morning at five, and toiled all day long —could Arthur sleep with the knowledge that *on her not dropping off to sleep the life of Edith depended?* Let those who have truly loved answer that question.

Edith lay still, "white as her sheets," when Arthur, with the rest of the family, retired—they for the night, he to spend the long hours in walking up and down before Edith's door, to listen whether Lisbeth was up and stirring, and whether she regularly administered the sustenance on which depended that young life, and, consequently, his own.

For some time (as the door was ajar) he had no difficulty in ascertaining that old Lisbeth, who kept on muttering to herself, did her duty well. He could hear her stirring, praising herself in guttural sounds, keeping up the fire, and feeding her patient as gently as a nursing-mother her babe. He could hear a few soft, weak, gentle words of thanks from Edith. But at the coldest, shortest, darkest hour that precedes the Dawn, he felt the air of his darling's room (as he stood at the door) grow chill. There was no longer a ruddy glow from the open fireplace (a great rarity, as we have said, but the villa belonged to an English family). Presently his heart grew cold and heavy, for he distinctly heard a loud, regular snore, and then all the blood in his body seemed to rush to his head and face, for he caught some low, imploring words of Edith. He thought she said, "Brandy, Lisbeth! a little brandy! Oh, haste! I sink—I die! Lisbeth, brandy!" And Lisbeth—horror of horrors!—locked in labour-earned sleep, only replied by another and louder snore! Then did faithful, sleepless, watchful Love win the right to enter that chamber, and the triumph of saving that priceless life!

Arthur stole to Edith's bedside; Arthur administered a teaspoonful of the cordial which the fainting girl craved and implored her snoring nurse for, and in vain! Arthur's arm supported the beloved form, upheld the beauteous head against his breast, while he cautiously held to her lips what, in this case, was indeed *eau de vie.* (How often has it proved, to those who do *not* need it, *eau de mort.* It is at once a *spirit* of evil and of good.)

After imbibing those few drops, a faint tinge of colour returned to the pale cheeks and lips. Edith raised the snowy lids, that had scarcely strength to lift the weight of the long brown lashes. The large blue eyes gleamed with love and joy, and then slowly filled with tears, as, her fair head drooping on his breast, she said,

"Heaven bless you, Arthur, my beloved!"

The nurse Lisbeth had dropped asleep in a chair by the fire, watching some broth, which had all boiled away before her closed eyes. Arthur made some attempts to arouse Lisbeth, but he soon saw that, even if he succeeded in awaking her, she would inevitably drop off again; and so he resolved to resume his watch at Edith's door. He did not like to take advantage of her unconscious and helpless state, to establish himself in the arm-chair by her bed; but he made up the fire, put on more broth, refilled the kettle, trimmed the lamp, and taking out his watch, placed it before him, with a lamp, on a little table outside Edith's door on the landing, as he established himself there.

Sounder and sounder slept old Lisbeth; and louder and louder became her regular snore. Every quarter of an hour, Arthur administered the necessary nourishment, in return for which he heard Edith bless him! Gradually the colour deepened on her cheeks and lips; her pulse became stronger, fuller, more regular; her breathing softer and freer.

Towards five o'clock (old Lisbeth's usual hour for rising) she began to stir, to snort, to groan, to stretch. Arthur saw she would soon be wide awake; and so, with a blessing and a prayer, he softly on tiptoe left the room.

Lisbeth yawned, rubbed her eyes, and was frightened at first to find she had fallen asleep; bnt when she saw the fire burning, the water boiling, and Edith looking so much better and less wan, she persuaded herself that she had only slept for a few minutes, and our lovers never undeceived her.

Arthur watched her for some time, until he felt certain that she had waked up full of energy, and better able to nurse sweet Edith than he was; for, the excitement and anxiety over, he found himself cramped with cold, and very, very weary.

But he had saved his darling's life; but for him, she must have died of exhaustion, as, alas! so many do, while hired nurses sleep. But she is saved—saved by Love and him! And with this conviction warm at his heart, Arthur hurried to his cold bed, and was soon fast asleep.

CHAPTER XXII.

" Oh, there's nothing half so sweet in life
As Love's young dream."

MOORE.

EDITH LORRAINE'S recovery was very rapid. Youth and a good constitution were on her side, and, better still, the delightful (though silent) conviction that she owed her life to Arthur's devotion. In the long hours of convalescence this thought cheered her drooping spirit, and sent the bloom to her cheek, and the love-light to her eye.

Lisbeth boasted of a recovery which she attributed solely to her unremitting care and *sleepless* tending during the night of the crisis. Yes, she boasted and triumphed, and was thanked, praised, rewarded. And our lovers kept their own counsel; only Arthur stole a timid glance at Edith, while Mrs. Croft was pompously presenting Lisbeth with a new dress, and Mr. Croft with a silver watch, for her successful tending of their dearest Edith; and the blushes that suffused Edith's face, neck, brow, and bosom, and the tears that gathered in her eyes as she gazed at Arthur, convinced him—though they had not yet had an opportunity of exchanging a word on the subject—that she was fully conscious to whom she owed her life, albeit a thousand maiden scruples kept her silent then.

This delightful secret formed a new bond of union between Arthur and Edith.

Woman's love is always half gratitude, while man's is often in a great measure made up of a sense of protecting the gentle, timid creature whose instincts teach her to look up to him, to cling to him, to cleave to him. As a little boy, Arthur had left rosy, merry little girls, to sit by Edith's reclining-board, when she was "the little carroty cripple"—the large-eyed, pale-faced, sharp-chinned, small, halting girl, whom everyone looked upon as certain to be humpbacked, but who was so grateful, so patient, so intelligent, and so pious.

"When we learn to pity, how soon we learn to love!"

says the poet. Arthur's first feelings for Edith were those of intense pity—pity that she could not run about the fields like the little Croft girls, to gather wild flowers, nor go nutting in the woods, nor ride the Shetland pony, nor sport by the wild sea, but must always be in a dull room, on her reclining-board, so lonely, except for him! Then, when he noted her patience, her faith, and her cheerfulness, a feeling of reverence, of admiration, and of deep tenderness, grew up in his heart. To her he brought the first snowdrop, the first primrose, the first violet, the first rose, the first red strawberry, or sunny apricot, or fragrant blackberry, the first golden wheatear. The little callow bird, fallen from its nest, was laid on a little table by her side; so was the velvet mole, which looked like a very old-fashioned lady, with a long nose, in a very tight-skirted velvet dress, pressed to death by too tight a belt. The deserted bird's nest was brought to her, and so were the pebbles, which, on the beach, looked like many-coloured gems, but seemed such poor, dull things, when they were spread before Edith.

Edith could scarcely remember the time when Arthur had not been her great solace, guide, companion, and friend; and Arthur felt that he had always loved Edith, but that he had never been *in love* with her till she was fifteen and he seventeen. And now, the stronger the passion that filled their young hearts, the more reserved were they in each other's company. Love, as in Lalla Rookh's case, had fled from their eyes, to hide himself in their hearts.

Edith was again a member of the family circle when Roger Croft arrived at Bellevue Villa, with his tutor, or "coach," as he called him, and with a gay party of young men of his college, travelling during the long vacation, among whom the young Lord Pontecraft was pre-eminent for wealth, rank, importance, and influence over his young companions. These Oxonions were all singularly alike; they were all dressed by one tailor, adorned by one jeweller, shod by one bootmaker; their hair was cut by one hairdresser, their hats came from one hatter—even their shirts, gloves, ties, collars, were all furnished by the same purveyor. They had been educated in one school—Eton; one college—

Christ Church; they were all close imitators of one model—the young Marquis, and all, except Roger Croft, were of the aristocracy. We say all except Roger, for in everything Arthur was as unlike as possible to the "set" now honouring the Bellevue Villa with their presence. They all thought the same thoughts, felt, or affected to feel, to think, to talk, walk, sit, loll, yawn, and smoke alike. They had one common slang—Oxford slang; one common drawl, one very bad slow walk, though they all aimed at being thought "fast." They all joined in quizzing Harkup Hackney, their "coach," whom the young Marquis set the fashion of calling "Old Hackney-Coach." Hackney was a first-rate scholar and mathematician—a "double first" who had lived from the age of eighteen to fifty-two the cloistered, monkish life of an Oxford private tutor, and who was as simple, absent, unworldly, credulous, and ignorant of the world and its ways as any village girl of fifteen. He was also as pure of heart, as impulsive and affectionate. He was engaged to be married, too, as soon as he had amassed a certain sum wherewith to make a settlement on the object of his affections—a curate's seventh daughter. This curate had been his schoolmaster; and Prudence Pryme and Harkup Hackney had been lovers from the time that he was a gaunt, plain, but very clever, kind-hearted boy, in jacket and turn-down collar, and Prudence a rosy hoyden, in white frock and frilled trousers, and with her golden hair hanging in ringlets down her back, till now, that his once long, wild black hair was iron grey, and till Time had stolen the gold from her locks, and left the change in silver.

Harkup Hackney was a tall, wiry, powerful man, with a parchment skin, deeply furrowed with the lines of thought. Like

Dominie Sampson, he paid no attention to his dress; but it was the delight of the young Marquis, who cared not what money he lavished on what he called "a lark," to substitute for old Hackney-Coach's threadbare black coat and washed-out trousers, whatever was gayest and most in fashion; and he, full of squaring the circle, or turning a Greek epigram, put on whatever he found on the chair by his bedside, and would have done so had it been a general's uniform, or a Chinese mandarin's robes.

For nearly thirty years Prudence Pryme and Harkup Hackney had been engaged. They had not often met in that long period; for old Pryme, the lady's father, lived at the very top of Northumberland, and Harkup had, considering the object he had in view, no money to spend in travelling; but they had constantly corresponded, and Harkup was, by extreme industry and self-denial, fast approaching the realisation of the sum old Pryme insisted on, before he would allow Prudence to marry. He had suffered such misery from wedded poverty himself—for he was a gentleman by birth, and had married a lady—that he vowed no *girl* of his should unite herself to a man who could not keep her in comfort, and settle on her enough to secure her a competency in case of widowhood.

Several times, at intervals of many years, Harkup Hackney had been all but ready, when the failure of some bank or some speculation, into which Craft had inveigled his Simplicity, threw him back again as far as ever from the altar and Prudence! He was, however, very near them now; and the sum he was to receive as travelling tutor to our party of "nobs" would all but enable him to present himself at the parsonage, near the Borders, to claim of the curate of eighty his grey-haired daughter of forty-nine—his old, old bride, who was still young in his eyes, and fair, too, for hard study had dimmed his sight, and the image of what she had been, was engraven on his heart; while the recollection of her constancy, her tenderness, and her truth made her, to him, the *beau ideal* of womankind.

END OF THE FIRST VOLUME.

CPSIA information can be obtained
at www.ICGtesting.com
Printed in the USA
LVHW100513130422
716029LV00002B/90

9 783752 593914